YOU

Other titles by Sandra Glover

YOU

Sandra Glover ©

Andersen Press • London

First published in 2003 by
Andersen Press Limited,
20 Vauxhall Bridge Road, London SW1V 2SA
www.andersenpress.co.uk

British Library Cataloguing in Publication Data available
ISBN 1 84270 168 1

Typeset by FiSH Books, London WC1
Printed and bound in Great Britain by Mackays of Chatham Ltd.,
Chatham, Kent

Chapter 1

I had to pick it up, didn't I? I couldn't just buy my chewing gum and walk out of there, could I? Not once I'd seen the headline.

Most of the heavy papers were leading on some new peace talks. A couple of the tabloids had done 'The game show love rat' but one paper, the one lying on the table in front of me now, had gone big on 'Is Law too soft on Young Offenders?'

'Decided yet?'

I nearly shoot out of my seat as the voice growls at me. The waiter must think I'm a right nutter. He stands, looking bored and irritated, as I pick up the plastic-covered card which passes as a menu.

'Er . . . a salad sandwich and a cappuccino, thanks.'

'That all?' he says, as though it was a waste of time coming over.

'Yes . . . thanks.'

He shrugs and slouches off and I can't help noticing what a nice bum he's got. He's nice all round really. Tall, despite the slouch, very slim hips, dark hair and olive skin like he might be Italian or something, though the accent's definitely Liverpool . . . or is it Birmingham? I've never been too good on accents. His face would be OK too if he didn't scowl so much and I wonder whether I could make him smile.

I think I could 'cos he winks at me as he hovers at the next table. He's definitely showing a bit of interest. But no. Leave it, Josie. He looks like a 'bad lad' – the sort Moira tells me I have to stay clear of. Along with the booze, the drugs and all the other stuff that could screw up my life. I guess Moira thinks I'm screwed up enough already without adding to my problems. And she's right. She's definitely right about that.

'Just concentrate on getting through your college course, Josie,' she tells me. 'Get a few more qualifications behind you.'

So I ignore the Liverpudlian-Brummie-Italian waiter and hide behind my newspaper. Reading the article again. Feeling my stomach twisting itself into knots and that point, just above my right eye, starting to throb.

The newspaper isn't what you'd call sympathetic to the wailings of the European Court of Human Rights or to the Home Secretary's latest reforms. It doesn't want young offenders working in the community and it certainly isn't keen on the reduced sentences.

In fact I get the impression that the paper and most of its readers would be happy to bring back the birch and the rope. Yeah...there's someone on the letters page actually suggesting it!

The newspaper's screaming that the law was already too soft, even before the latest changes and they've dragged up all the old cases again to make their point.

2

The fifteen-year-old lad who robbed a pensioner and who not only got off but claimed compensation because the pensioner bashed him over the head with his walking stick.

'Outrageous!' the paper says.

That boy who assaulted his teacher, successfully suing his school because they failed to provide for his 'special needs'.

'Where's the justice in that?' the paper asks.

The old Thompson and Venables case. They've even dragged up the Mary Bell affair from the middle of the last century! Just how long does it take for them to leave people alone?

Not that they've skimped on the more recent stuff. They've gone mega big on the fact that you've been released early, Alex.

And their poor readers are worried, the paper claims. Where exactly have you been released to? What if you happen to be living in their town? Their street? Would they be safe? Would their children be safe?

Probably not because over sixty per cent of released young offenders go on to re-offend, the paper says. Frightening statistic that, if it's true.

'Salad sandwich. Cappuccino. Now, you sure I can't get you anything else, luv?'

I can't help it. I jump again and the waiter thinks it's him who's having this electric effect on me I reckon, 'cos he winks and smiles this time.

'No. Nothing.'

I stress the nothing. He gets the point and wanders

off. So that's great. That's my girl, Josie! Don't be tempted by the bad boys.

Trouble is, I can't go for the nice boys either. There's this lad at college. Graham, he's called. I try to sit behind him when I can. Sometimes he turns round and smiles, so I know he likes me. But that's only because he doesn't know me. And I'm not really sure I want him to. I don't want anybody getting too close.

That's one of the reasons I keep myself to myself. Come into town to eat, rather than use the facilities at college. Use a different place almost every day. So no one gets to notice me much. No one starts getting too friendly, asking questions.

Even simple questions throw me sometimes.

'Where do you come from, then?'

'Got any brothers or sisters?'

Scary. Most people probably don't clock how many questions they're asked in a day. To most people, questions are just questions. To me they're land mines waiting to blow up in my face. Because there's no way I can tell the truth, is there? And lying's harder than you might think. Oh, I know lying came easy enough to you, Alex. As natural as breathing. But it doesn't to me. Big lies, massive lies, are hard to remember, so I'm always terrified I'm going to make a mistake.

I sip my coffee and get as far as nibbling a corner of my sandwich before I realize I've missed something in the paper. It's not just the front page, page 2, page 3 and the letters page. There's another article on page 14.

They've done interviews with some of the families, friends and neighbours of the victims.

Your victims, Alex! And I have to move my coffee and sandwich and lay the paper flat on the table 'cos it's shaking so much in my hands.

The things they say they'd do to you if they found you! Not that they will. You're well protected, I reckon, and that's another thing the paper's ranting about. How much it costs to keep people like you inside. How much more they have to spend on you for years and years after your release.

Not only on the offenders themselves either, the article helpfully points out. Members of their family often need help, therapy, counselling. All at the taxpayers' expense, don't you know?

Then, of course, the families, as well as the offenders, have to be re-housed, re-named, protected. Otherwise they get the bricks through the windows, don't they? The spray-painted death threats on the walls, the lighted paper through the letter box.

Why do I get the feeling that the paper and its readers would be quite happy to save a bit of money and leave them to their fate, at the hands of the revenge seekers, the vigilantes, the nutters?

Maybe because of the tone of the rest of the article. Maybe because of the words they use to describe you, Alex! 'Evil', 'psychotic', 'an animal', 'deranged', 'mad', 'disgusting', 'vile', 'unnatural'.

For a moment, for one mad moment, I want to leap up, wave the paper around, scream out that they've got it all wrong. It wasn't like that. YOU weren't like that.

But I don't. Because the trouble is, Alex, they're right. I'd like to defend you, part of me thinks I should, but I can't. Not even to myself.

'Don't look at me like that!'

'Sorry?' says the waiter, swinging round.

'Er . . . nothing,' I say.

How can I explain that I wasn't talking to him? How can I tell him I was talking to you?

It's getting worse. It's definitely getting worse. At first I only used to see you at night. Bad dreams. Nightmares, when I'd wake up screaming for you to go away, leave me alone.

Then you started popping up at other times.

'It's OK,' one of my counsellors said when I told her. 'These things happen, in cases like yours. But once you start to face up to things, once you've talked it all through, these hallucinations will pass, I promise you.'

But they haven't. Well, maybe they did for a while. But since your release, eight months ago, they've got stronger. More scary. Threatening. Like you're trying to tell me you'll find a way back. Come bursting into my life again, leading me astray. Wrecking everything like you always did.

'That part of your life is behind you now,' Moira tells me sometimes. 'You have to move on, Josie. Alex . . . what happened back then . . . it's over now. Finished. You have to start believing that, Josie.'

And I'd like to believe her. I'd like to do what she says.

6

But how can I when you conjure yourself up at all times of the day and night? Haunting me like this!

I did Shakespeare for GCSE and A-levels. Can you imagine that? Me doing exams? Me reading Shakespeare? But it wasn't boring, like you'd think. It was dead good. Both the plays we did, *Macbeth* and *Hamlet*, had ghosts in them. And my teacher said that Shakespeare wrote about ghosts because people believed in them in those days and that we had to use our imaginations a bit. Pretend that we lived in dark, superstitious times and believed in them too.

But I didn't have to pretend. About the dark times. About the ghosts. I knew just how Hamlet felt when he saw his father prowling round the ramparts of that castle. I knew why Macbeth flipped when he saw Banquo sitting there at the table all battered and bleeding.

Because I see you all the time.

Crazy. Malicious. Grinning that manic smile of yours.

Oh sure, they tell me you're not like that now. That you've changed. Seen the error of your ways. Shown remorse. That you're not a danger to anyone anymore. Otherwise they wouldn't have let you out, would they?

Well, I hope they're right, Alex. I hope you can be trusted out in the big wild world. I'm not so sure. And, even if you're not a danger to anyone else, you're still a danger to me. You always will be.

Locked up or on the loose, it doesn't make much difference to me. You're always there. Taunting me. Reminding me about what happened. Trying to make out it was my fault. But it wasn't! It was yours, Alex. Your fault, not mine.

'So leave me alone!'

The middle-aged couple on the next table turn to look at me. And I know I've done it again. Spoken out loud.

This is what happens, isn't it, Alex? I've only got to start thinking about you and I start acting weird. That's how strong you are. Even with all the help I've had, there's a part of me that can't block you out. A part that sees you still.

And it doesn't really help to live in the twenty-first century. To know that the ghosts aren't real, that the darkness is all inside. You're not even dead, are you, Alex? No such luck. So I know you're not a real ghost. But that only makes it worse. To know that I'm conjuring you up myself.

I blink. Try so hard to shut you out. But I can't. You're still there, Alex. Part of my life. Part of my past. Casting your dark shadow over my present, my future.

And it reminds me of that crazy game we used to play when we were infants. Running round the playground, trying to get rid of our shadows.

I couldn't do it then and I can't do it now.

And the worst of it is, you look so real sitting there, grinning, drawing me back, drawing me in.

Any minute now you'll lean forward, start whispering. Telling me what you remember. Making me remember too.

Chapter 2

You were always the really crazy one. Even by the standards of our estate, our school. What was our class like, eh? Talk about wild. Right from infants we'd have a new teacher every three months or so because the old one had got sacked or had a nervous breakdown. Sometimes both.

I don't think there was a kid in there who didn't have some sort of problem. Unemployed parents doing their best to bring them up on benefits. Parents who'd turned to crime to pay the bills and ended up in prison. Families who were the victims of crime. Depressed families. Sick families. Oh they tried, I suppose. But I guess it's not that easy when there are no jobs, no money, nothing much to look forward to.

The stresses led to a lot of people splitting up, I reckon, 'cos there were loads of broken families. Broken! What am I saying? Some of us had homes that had been broken up so often, our family trees looked like jigsaw puzzles.

Not that any of the teachers were daft enough to ask us to draw a family tree. Far too risky with Joey's dad living with Hari's mum whose first husband had taken up with Jason's seventeen-year-old sister. Trying to disentangle who belonged to who would have started a riot.

It took a whole lot less than that to start a riot usually. Most days were chaos. There'd be the kids with Attention Deficit Disorder clambering on the tables and chucking chairs around. The one with Tourette's syndrome yelling the F-word, the C-word and a whole lot of B-words that aren't in the dictionary. While the dozen or so who wanted to get on with their work tried and usually failed.

Trouble was, the quiet kids, the more normal kids, sort of got pushed into the background, didn't they? With people like you acting up for attention all the time. Even worse, you'd eventually get some of them joining in, wouldn't you? Dragging everyone down with you. Bit of a speciality of yours, was that.

And do you know why, Alex? Because you were jealous. Don't bother trying to deny it. You were, you know. Jealous of the clever kids, the happy kids, anyone who was doing well. That's why you tried to spoil it for them, with your acting up, fooling around and your bullying.

Most kids were a bit scared of you. Some were absolutely terrified. Like poor Tyrone. Knees pulled up to his chest, rocking and nodding to himself, hands over his ears trying to block out the noise, as you stood there, yelling and swearing at the teacher. Tyrone was autistic, I think. Or was he Asperger's?

Of course I didn't know all those fancy words and syndromes at the time. Didn't really know there was anything wrong with us at all. I just thought most of us were normal kids. Bit excitable, bit rowdy but perfectly normal, thank you very much.

It's only looking back, with all the jargon I've learnt since, through my therapy and counselling and stuff, that I can start to match up the various symptoms with some of my own classmates.

I'm not sure though, even now, that they've come up with the right terms or syndromes to describe you. Bit of a one-off, you were.

Other kids could get the teachers shouting, raving, trembling, gibbering but only you could make them physically sick. Like that time when you were still only in Year 3 and they found that hedgehog on the school field. Or what was left of the hedgehog. Namely a few charred and blackened spikes in an old biscuit tin.

Someone, I'm not sure who, let on it had something to do with you, a can of siphoned-off petrol and a stolen cigarette lighter.

'Why do you do these things, Alex?' Mrs Kerr had asked, shaking her head.

'I didn't, miss!' you said, looking at her out of eyes so huge and blue and innocent that she was tempted to believe you.

You had your head shaved then, I seem to remember. Trying to look hard. But whatever you did to yourself you never quite managed to lose that baby look. And, although you hated it, it could sure come in handy at times.

'I didn't, miss,' you repeated. 'I wouldn't do nothing like that. Not to an animal. I like animals.'

She was wavering. Oh yes, she was wavering. She

11

wanted to believe you. Only it was tricky because of the three witnesses who claimed to have seen you. Three 'nice' kids from Year 6.

'Oh, Alex, why?' Mrs Kerr said again.

I don't think Mrs Kerr got an answer. How could she? You wouldn't have known, would you? You wouldn't have known why you did it. You never did.

'Look, Alex,' she said, trying another track. 'I'm not saying it was you, all right. It might have been or it might not have been. But I want you to think about that poor creature. I want you to try to understand what it must have suffered. What agony it went through being burnt alive like that. Do you understand what I'm saying, Alex?'

You nodded.

'So can you tell me, Alex? Can you tell me what that poor little animal felt like?'

'Hot,' you said.

She slapped you across the face. Someone ran off to tell the Head and that was the end of Mrs Kerr.

She'd misunderstood, though, hadn't she? She thought you were trying to be funny or cheeky. She didn't know you. She'd only been there a couple of months. Supply teacher, I think she was.

Not all the things you did were sick. Most of them were well funny. You fancied yourself as the class clown, didn't you? You were the one who left the drawing pins on the teacher's chair. You were the one who put that big plastic frog down the loo and the real slug in Sunita's lunch box.

Then there was the time in Year 4, when you turned up with your arm all bandaged, in a sling, and said you'd fallen off the garage roof. It was your right arm too, so you couldn't do any work, not for ages. Weeks and weeks. And everyone felt dead sorry for you. Until Vince Matthews tried to push past you in the lunch queue and you got mad and laid into him. With your right arm!

'Yeah, well, my arm's better now,' you told the dinner lady.

Only, it hadn't ever been broken in the first place, had it?

Funnily enough, when you used a similar trick a couple of months later, nobody realized, did they? You could get away with...

No. I won't say it. Not really appropriate, is it? Appropriate. I know all the big words now.

We didn't back then. Maybe it would have helped if we'd gone to school a bit more often. But we didn't. None of us were what you'd call regular attenders.

You certainly weren't. I don't think you ever meant to skip school. 'Cos most of the time you didn't mind it, really. It was a bit of a laugh, school. It's just that you were hopeless at getting up in the mornings and by the time you'd crawled out of bed it never seemed worth going, did it?

Sometimes you'd stay home watching telly, playing video games, while your mum slept off a hangover. If you heard her getting up you'd sneak out and maybe wander down town. There'd always be someone around.

Someone else who was bunking off. Someone else whose parents either didn't know or didn't care.

Big gangs of us would get together sometimes, especially in summer. We'd wander round the shops, nicking sweets and cans of drink. The shopkeepers would know what we were up to. But they never caught us at it. We had a system. You got everyone organized, properly. Like the Mafia or a Chinese Triad, you used to say. I suppose you got it all from the films you watched. You were into old kung fu films around then, I seem to remember. Eight years old we were and already into petty crime!

Anyway, it all came to a bit of a stop at the end of Year 4. The school had some government inspectors in and I don't reckon they were too impressed. We had a talk in assembly and letters got sent home about the importance of regular attendance, hard work and co-operation from families.

I don't expect many people read the letters or listened that much in assembly. I think we all thought things would go on much the same as before. But we were wrong. In September, at the start of Year 5, they got a new head in. Mrs Wallace. 'The Dragon', you called her.

Even you were a bit scared of her, on the quiet. Within weeks she'd got rid of all our tables and replaced them with single desks set out in rows. She bought boxes of blue sweatshirts with the school's name printed on them and made us all wear them. If anyone couldn't afford to buy them, or claimed they couldn't, they got them for free. If we didn't turn up for school she came knocking

14

on our doors or drove down town and rounded us up.

We all got fed up after a while and took to coming in on our own. Though why she wanted some of us there, I can't imagine.

Especially you. The place would have been a whole lot quieter without you. Some people say The Dragon worked miracles. The school passed the next inspection and I've heard it's crept right up near the middle of them league table things now. So maybe the younger kids, all the little ones coming through, got used to her. But we didn't.

We all hated her. You more than most. We hated the way she'd come prowling round the classrooms, making sure we were all doing our work, or at least sitting safely in our seats. She had a way of shouting that wasn't really shouting at all. More like a loud whisper! But it really put the fear into us. Most of the teachers could turn blue with rage and we'd just laugh. But nobody laughed at The Dragon.

Even worse than the whispered shout was when she tried to be nice and jolly. Every assembly was treated like the flaming Oscars. Good work was held up and read out, while The Dragon beamed down at us and led the applause. There were certificates for good behaviour. Class awards. Individual awards. 'The Good Neighbour' shield. 'The Attendance Trophy'.

Some of the younger kids were really taken in, weren't they? Desperate to have their names read out. Greedy for that bar of chocolate that went with the certificates. But not us. We knew better. We knew what she was up to.

You organized a little club, didn't you? Called the F.A. club. The second word was awards and the first was a bit rude! The rules were simple. Anyone could join as long as they never ever got one of The Dragon's stupid awards. The minute anyone did, they were out.

You thought you were pretty safe, didn't you? Oh, you were smart enough, compared to a lot there, but I don't think you ever finished a piece of work and, of course, a 'good behaviour award' was out of the question.

But we all have our little weaknesses and yours was football. Bit of a blow when The Dragon introduced the 'Sports Personality Award', wasn't it? What were you supposed to do with the football season well underway and your six goals against Parkside already the talking point of the school?

You did the only thing you could do, short of giving up your precious football completely. You started missing practices, mucking around when you were there, missing open shots in matches.

Only when you knew it was safe though. When the team was already 3 up. You weren't going to go as far as throwing the whole match, were you? You couldn't stand to lose. So that was your downfall. The crucial cup final near the end of the Easter term.

It was against that snobby lot from Eastmoor Primary, who were all set to make it three cup wins in a row. Score one all, with two minutes to go. You yell at Vince Matthews to pass and he actually gets it right for once.

16

You go past one defender, then another and a third. By this time, the keeper's in a flap and he's come right out of his goal. You can't miss. Even Vince couldn't miss a shot like that. The killer instinct took over, I guess. You didn't stop to think, did you? You just belted it in and everyone went wild.

I say everyone. School matches didn't exactly draw massive crowds. It was hardly Old Trafford. But The Dragon was there snapping away with her camera.

Boy, did she make a big deal of it. Come Monday we had prints on the notice boards, mock newspaper reports and the cup in prime position in the new display cupboard she'd set up in the foyer.

You had your work cut out that week, didn't you? Doing everything you could to get into trouble. Swearing at the teachers, kicking a couple of infants in the playground, throwing a plate of spaghetti at one of the dinner ladies.

Everybody in our little club knew what you were up to. Make such a pain of yourself that no one in their right mind would give you any award whatsoever come Friday morning.

Only The Dragon clearly wasn't in her right mind. At least we didn't think so at the time. Now I understand why she did it. She thought she was building up your confidence. Praising your strengths not condemning your weaknesses. Encouraging you!

A few jaws dropped when she announced the 'Sports Personality Award'.

'I know Alex doesn't often win awards,' she said, to hoots of laughter. 'But this award isn't about being a good writer or artist. It's not even about being well behaved. It's about sporting achievement. And nobody has done more than Alex to boost the school's sports record. Second in the league and now Cup Winners, for the very first time in the school's history, I think. So let's give Alex a big round of applause.'

Sick as a parrot. That's what they say, isn't it? And that's how you looked, crawling out there, head down, dreading the glances of fellow club members. Only they weren't fellow members now, were they? Because you were out. Out of your own club.

Halfway down the assembly hall, you changed though, didn't you? Head went up, right arm punched the air and you positively snatched the certificate and chocolate bar. Turning round. Holding them up. Looking dead chirpy and proud.

The Dragon looked proud too. Proud of you. Proud of herself. She thought she'd won, didn't she?

She didn't know you tore the certificate into tiny, tiny pieces on the way home, did she? You ate the chocolate though. Said it was stupid to waste it. You said something else too. You said the rules of our club had changed. It was OK to get a certificate, as long as you did something afterwards. If you could get your own back on The Dragon within a week of getting an award, you could stay in the club.

It was a great rule that. Kept us entertained right to the

end of Year 5 and through to Year 6, that one did. Everyone tried to copy you. Get an award, then try to do something awful to The Dragon within a week. Most didn't manage the second part and, in the end, the club had so few members left it wasn't worth it.

But you managed to stay in. Four of those blasted sports awards, I think you got, and four times you managed to upset The Dragon in a big way. But that first time was the best.

Everyone was watching you that next week, wondering what you were going to do. They hadn't clicked that The Dragon had actually made it easy.

One of her big aims was to get us kids more involved with the life of the school. She'd made up all these stupid jobs for us to do. Just like the awards, there were rotas and monitors for everything. Milk monitors, register monitors, litter monitors, book monitors.

Slavery, you called it and, of course, you didn't volunteer or let any members of the club volunteer to be monitors. But the rotas were different. They weren't voluntary. Everybody's name was bunged on some rota or other. Anyone who had a preference could choose but club members, naturally, didn't fancy anything, so our names got shoved on any rota where there were spaces.

You were put on the 'hospitality' rota. Basically it meant that every time there were parents, governors or some other posh visitor in school, the people on the hospitality rota went to the staff room with a classroom assistant to make coffee and little cakes or something.

As luck would have it, the Wednesday after you got the dreaded award, the Mayor was coming in to have a look round and talk to The Dragon.

She'd already told us it was important, something about getting some extra money for the school. So we needed to make a good impression. Oh yeah!

People should have smelt something a bit fishy when you insisted on changing rota places with Amrit and went off with Mrs Curtis and Dopey David Davenport to the staff room.

You were always dead lucky. Anybody else would have got Mrs Bell who had eyes like an eagle and a temperament to match. You got Mrs Curtis who was useless with a capital U.

Better still, Mrs Curtis had Dopey David to cope with, who couldn't even be trusted to pick a cup up without dropping it.

You had your plan all worked out, as you told people later. You'd brought in some very special ingredients to put in those nice little cakes. Bit of a problem when Dopey David dropped the flour, though, because it was the very last bag and Mrs Curtis didn't fancy scraping it all up off the staff room carpet.

Mrs Curtis was rushing around in a panic, wondering if it was all right to offer the Mayor a couple of stale biscuits instead or whether she had time to nip to the shops.

Meanwhile you were having a look in the fridge. Shop-bought biscuits didn't fit in with your plan at all.

'There's some bread and cheese,' you said. 'We could do toasted sandwiches. That'd be easy.'

'Good idea, Alex,' said Mrs Curtis. 'We can cut them into lovely little triangles, can't we? Now, David, would you like to help me sort out the coffee machine while Alex slices some cheese.'

You took your time because they weren't needed till 10.30. Laid all the ingredients out ready. Well, perhaps not quite all of them.

'Can I make the sandwiches on my own?' you asked. 'I've used a machine like this before.'

Whether you had or you hadn't didn't really matter. They're simple enough those things. Even you could have worked it out from scratch. Lift the lid. Put slice of bread inside. Add cheese and secret ingredient. Pop another slice of bread on top. Close lid. Switch on. Wait for light to go off and bell to ping. Repeat for sandwich two. Meanwhile cut sandwich one into nice little triangles, like Mrs Curtis said. Arrange on plate. Repeat for sandwich two.

The only problem, as far as you were concerned, was that once you and Dopey David had delivered the coffee and sandwiches to The Dragon's lair, you had to go back to class. You weren't allowed to hang around. So you never got to see their reaction.

'You didn't!' members of our club squealed as they gathered round you at break, listening to your story. 'You didn't never put worms in them sandwiches. Not real worms!'

You had though. The Dragon herself confirmed it. Funnily enough she seemed more concerned about the worms than the fact that The Mayor had puked up on her office carpet.

Bit like the hedgehog, I suppose. The worms wouldn't have enjoyed being toasted any more than the hedgehog enjoyed being burnt. But you couldn't see that, could you? The rest of the class did, once it had been spelt out to them. They all stopped laughing when The Dragon pointed out that it was a dangerous and cruel thing to do. Dangerous to the people. Cruel to the worms.

But you still didn't get it, I reckon. You just wouldn't have known how those worms felt.

I do. I know how the worms felt and I know how The Dragon and the Mayor must have felt when they realized what was in their mouths, their throats, their stomachs.

It's put me right off my salad sandwich, just thinking about it.

Time to go anyway. That waiter's been staring at me again. Or is it you he's staring at? Can he see you sitting there too?

Probably not. Could anyone else at that feast see Banquo? No way. Because Macbeth's ghosts came from inside too. But it doesn't make them any less real, does it?

You look happy now. Now you've made me focus on you again, instead of getting on with my own life. So what next? Are you going to jump back into the box marked 'the past', where you belong? Or are you going to follow me back to college? I don't want to be late. We've got someone from the RSPCA coming in this afternoon to show us how to handle exotic species.

I'm doing animal welfare at college, Alex.

What do you make of that, eh?

Chapter 3

College is dead good. It's not all reading and writing, though I quite enjoy that sort of stuff now. We have practical sessions, like this one. To get us used to handling different kinds of animals. This guy from the RSPCA's brought in a python, a lizard, a pair of rats, a buzzard and a tarantula. All the things people have phobias about.

The snake got most people going. Almost put me off Graham, it did, seeing him break out into a sweat the minute the python was lifted out of its basket. Wimp or what? He managed to put a brave face on it though, touching the snake, stroking it, even picking it up in the end.

I didn't have any trouble with the snake. Didn't have any trouble with anything. And if I went a bit pale when the tarantula was crawling up my arm, it wasn't what people thought. I'm not scared of spiders. Never have been. It's just that the tarantula reminded me of you . . . in more ways than one.

The way you used to catch flies, moths, beetles, butterflies and pop them into webs, watching them struggle until the spider came racing out.

Funny the way people distinguish between different types of animal, isn't it? If it was flies or beetles you were feeding to the spiders, people would laugh and watch. If

24

it was butterflies, they'd moan at you, say you were sick, especially if it was one of the really pretty ones. A Red Admiral or one of those things with orange tips on their wings.

It's the same with food. Brits are quite happy to tuck into roast lamb or beef burgers but suggest a dog casserole or a nice piece of grilled horse and they get all upset.

It was one of the things I found dead confusing once I'd got to thinking about it. It came up in some of my therapy sessions. The rights and wrongs of killing things. And I couldn't really get it. I'm not sure I do now. That's why I don't bother with meat of any sort anymore. So I don't have to think about it. I've got enough things to worry about, without constantly fretting about what's going into my mouth. Like my obsession with you. Why can't I just get rid of you, Alex? Why can't I forget? Why can't I just let it go?

'Ooooh, get it away from me! Take it away!'

Whoops. Soppy Sarah's flipped over the tarantula. She wasn't keen on the lizard or snake either. Makes you wonder what she's doing on an animal course in the first place. Graham wonders too. He grins at me and I can't help smiling back.

Sarah's making such a performance of it. Edging forward, stretching out her hand to touch the spider. Leaping back, shrieking. Fascinated and horrified at the same time.

And that's the other reason the tarantula reminds me of you. That's the sort of effect you had on people, wasn't

25

it? Fascination. Horror. No one ever quite knowing what you'd do next. Always hanging around to watch, always getting sucked in, whether they really wanted to or not.

Like the time when you were nine and you tied little Liam Bradbury onto the roundabout on the green, spinning it round faster and faster, till he was screaming and crying, completely hysterical. And no one was really sure whether it was a game or not, least of all you. So when you told them to take over, spin it round, they did, didn't they?

Not daring to stop, even when Liam started puking up, spraying mushy cornflakes and murky brown milk all over the place...because you were standing on one of the swings, laughing like some drug-crazed sergeant major, yelling at everyone to spin it faster...till your mum came out.

Our estate, our street, was what most people would call 'rough', though it wasn't as bad as some places. The houses were council semis built back in the 1950s and, as old Granny Newson, who lived at number 14 and was about a million years old, used to mutter through her loose-fitting false teeth:

'It were a nice place then. We could go out at night without fear of being mugged and no one ever bothered to lock their doors.'

According to Granny Newson people had nice gardens then too, not junk yards full of clapped-out cars, broken fridges and rusty bikes. The green in the middle wasn't full of dog poo and kiddies used to be able to play

26

safely on swings that weren't broken, a roundabout that wasn't covered in obscene graffiti, and without the fear of picking up needles and used condoms from underneath the slide.

But, then again, Granny Newson was a demented old cow, as you often used to tell her.

Anyway she had her beak pressed up against the window that day you had Liam Bradbury tied to the roundabout and your mum came out. It was probably Granny Newson who phoned your mum in the first place 'cos it was only about 11-ish on Saturday morning and it was obvious your mum had been in bed 'cos she appeared in her black nightie and slippers and all the lads turned and whistled as the nightie blew up above her knees.

'Alex!' she yelled, ignoring them. 'What the bloody hell are you doing?'

Come to think of it, she probably used stronger language than that. She usually did.

You leapt down off the swing and that was the cue for the few people who were still gamely pushing the roundabout to stop. Someone, I think it was Tracey, untied little Liam who scrambled off the roundabout, stood swaying for a second or two like a bemused Bambi and fell flat on his face.

Your mum, who'd had her arm outstretched, all set to belt you round the head, suddenly shrieked, threw back the tangle of blonde hair which flopped round her face and started howling with laughter in a way that set us all off.

27

'Oh, Alex,' she said, pulling you towards her, clutching you in a manic hug, while her whole, not exactly slim, body wobbled and shook. 'You are an eejit. Just look what you've done!'

She let go of you and helped the vomit-stained Liam to his feet.

'You're OK,' she told him. 'Stop snivelling. You're not hurt. Just a bit dizzy, that's all. Go on. Go and play.'

And poor Liam wandered off dazed and stupid towards the slide with everyone still shrieking, hooting and laughing.

You and your mum walked back together to your house, with Granny Newson watching and, no doubt, tutting behind her window. You stuck two fingers up as you passed.

You didn't care what anyone else said about your mum, and believe me they said a lot! You knew she was OK. All the kids in the close liked your mum. She was like a big kid herself most of the time, coming out, hurling handfuls of sweets around or sitting on the garden wall, playing her music loud and sharing bags of pale, greasy chips.

A lot of the men liked her too but it wasn't for her sweets and chips. That day, as you reached your house, a bloke appeared, half naked, in the open doorway. I don't remember who it was. Not your dad, that was for sure.

'I had a dad once,' you used to tell people proudly, when you were little. 'He was a bastard.'

And, as you got older, you'd come out with other bits of information too. Like his name...Alexander...and the fact that he left the day before your third birthday... just an hour before the cops turned up, wanting to talk to him about drug dealing and a bloke who'd been knifed outside a pub.

You never saw him again and your memories of him were vague but he'd left you with a few permanent reminders of himself, hadn't he? Like the tiny scars on your back where the cigarettes had burned and the ridges on your thighs where the belt buckle had cut in.

'Look at the state of this kid!' one of the cops had said, picking you up screaming as you tried to hold onto your mum.

You were taken into care for a few months but they let you go home, once it was clear your dad was never coming back. Because it was Daddy who had hurt you. Not Mummy. And once Daddy had gone Mummy promised she'd lay off the booze and try to look after you better, didn't she?

Anyway, that day of the roundabout business, the guy who wasn't your dad was looking pretty wound up and impatient. He snarled something at your mum, pushed her inside the house and slammed the door in your face.

You made out like you didn't care. And maybe you didn't. Maybe you were used to it. You just bounced back across the green, yelling orders, getting everyone organized into two teams for a game of footy.

You were always the organizer, always the leader. That was something that came out at your trial. That and a whole load of other things about your 'upbringing' or lack of it. Deprived. Emotionally damaged. Psychotic personality. A whole dictionary full of terms that could have applied to any number of kids, I suppose. But they didn't all do what you did, did they?

So it wasn't much of a defence and there was no way the jury was ever going to fall for 'the poor little victim routine'. Not with the families of all the real victims screaming for blood.

'It's bitten me! It's bitten me. I'm bleeding.'

Sarah's dancing round the room, shaking her hand, sucking her finger, examining a supposedly massive wound that no one else can see. And the white rat is back, hunched up in its cage, looking even more traumatized than Sarah. Wondering what it's done wrong. Aren't you allowed to bite if someone's got you in a stranglehold, squeezing the life out of you?

The answer is no, of course. Violence, retaliation, is always wrong. Not that we knew that when we were kids. It's something I learnt later. But I don't suppose that poor rat's ever had the benefit of counselling, has it?

'You have to be more gentle,' the RSPCA man's telling Sarah. 'Try not to panic. Watch.'

He gets the other rat, the silvery grey one, out of the cage and hands it to me.

'See how Josie does it,' he says and I feel myself burning up, as everyone turns to watch me.

This isn't what I want at all. How am I supposed to keep a low profile if the teachers start singling me out? But the soft fur feels warm and comforting on my hand and I can't help stroking the rat, letting it climb up my chest, where it stays with its little black nose twitching, perfectly relaxed and trusting.

'You see, they won't hurt you if you handle them properly,' the man tells Sarah.

And, as Sarah stares at me, all sort of jealous like, I feel a bit of a cheat. 'Cos it's not as though any of this comes naturally to me. It's something else I was taught during counselling, at the animal therapy centre, where we had cuddly bunnies to play with and hamsters and gerbils. All strictly supervised, of course. Good job, really. 'Cos I was dead rough and clumsy at first. Worse than Sarah.

But animal therapy's good. It's used all over the place. In hospitals, in old people's homes, with disabled children, with people who are traumatized. I don't think it's used much in prisons but it should be. The Home Secretary should bung that in his reforms somewhere. Pets would be good for criminals.

You can tell things to an animal that you'd never, ever say to a person. Because bunnies aren't easily shocked. As long as you feed them and cuddle them, they'll love you, even when you tell them your secrets.

And my silvery rat would still nuzzle into my neck even if I whispered in its ear, 'Seven years ago, Ratty, when we were just eleven years old, do you know what happened? What Alex did—'

But I won't because my whisper would carry round the room. Sarah and Graham and the RSPCA man and the others would stop and listen to the story. Wondering what it all had to do with me. And when they realized, they wouldn't be as understanding, as forgiving as you, Ratty. Oh, no.

I don't really want to give Ratty back but the session's winding up already and Sarah's going to have one last try, on her own, when the rest of us have gone.

'You were brill, Josie. Especially with that snake.'

I recognize Graham's voice, even before I turn round.

'I'm not too good with snakes,' he adds, somewhat unnecessarily.

'You did OK,' I say. 'Better than Sarah!'

'Yeah. She's going to have a bit of a hard time, isn't she? Look, I've been wondering, I've been meaning to ask,' he says all dead shy and polite. 'Do you fancy coming for a drink sometime?'

'Yes,' I say, when what I mean is no.

'Tonight?' he says.

Excuse, Josie. Make up an excuse.

But my head's already nodded.

'8 o'clock in the college bar?'

'Not the bar.'

Great, I've finally managed to say something I actually mean. But he looks bemused.

'I don't really like the bar,' I say by way of explanation.

'Neither do I! How about the new wine bar in town? Is 8 o'clock OK? Not too early?'

I nod and shake my head.

'Great,' he says. 'See you there.'

And he bounces off, looking genuinely pleased with himself, and I can't help wondering if he'd look quite so pleased if he knew.

Chapter 4

It's a ten-minute bus journey followed by a thirty-minute train journey and a five-minute walk home. Close enough to the college for me to commute but far enough away to keep my home life, such as it is, private, separate.

Sometimes I read on the journey but today I entertained myself counting how many houses had got their Christmas trees and decorations up already. The shops have had them up since August, or at least it seems that way, but not many houses have yet.

Mine hasn't. Just the normal light which shines night and day above the porch. I say my house, but it's not really. I just rent a room. But at least it's not one of those grotty purpose-built student hostels or anything. It's a three-storey Victorian terrace on a long tree-lined avenue. Dead posh really.

As far as the neighbours are concerned, Frank and Moira, who own the house, take in students. Nothing unusual in that. There's a couple of colleges near here and plenty of people rent out rooms to students to make a bit of extra cash.

Only Frank and Moira's students are a bit different from other people's. Frank and Moira's students are special. Youngsters who are too old for foster care but who, for one reason or another, need a bit of extra help. Who aren't 'safe' to be let loose on their own.

They've got four letting rooms but only two inmates, at the moment. Me and Lara. Lara has Down's syndrome and, though she can look after herself pretty well, she needs a lot of support with her college course.

She's very touchy-feely is Lara. Always gives me a big hug when she sees me, which really freaked me at first but now I sort of like it. She likes to stroke my hair sometimes too, which is even freakier, but I let her do it 'cos I don't want to upset her.

I think I did upset her a couple of times, early on. 'Cos I was scared of her. That's really horrible, isn't it? Being scared of someone just 'cos they look a bit different. I mean it's not as though looks have anything to do with what's inside, is it? If looks were anything to go by, you'd have been up for sainthood, wouldn't you, Alex? And Lara's not dangerous, no way! She's got that really cheerful, happy, smiley nature that Moira says often goes with Down's syndrome. Lucky for Lara really 'cos I don't reckon she's got much to be happy about.

Moira doesn't say much. It's part of the job to be discreet but I know Lara's been in care since she was two years old, which can't have been a whole bundle of fun, can it?

Anyway with Lara's 'special needs' and the way things are with me, Moira's not taking on anyone else at the moment.

She's made me a veggie-mince shepherd's pie! I recognize the smell the minute I walk through the door.

35

It'll be served with peas and a slice of beetroot. I know that because Moira's meals are very predictable. Good but predictable.

At weekends I do my own cooking, which consists mainly of fried egg and beans on toast and I'm supposed to do all my own cleaning and laundry. But Moira's dead good and often shoves some of my stuff in the washing machine or irons a few of my bits and pieces with her own. She's the same with Lara.

I'm not sure it's the best way to encourage us to become independent but I appreciate it 'cos I'm usually dead knackered when I come home from college. And besides, it seems to have worked OK with Moira's own kids, didn't it? They're all grown up with good jobs and families of their own. Their photographs beam down at me from nearly every wall and surface in the house, making me envy them. There were only ever two small photos of me on display at home and I expect even they've gone now.

'You OK, Josie?' Moira says as I sit down. 'You look a bit pale.'

'I'm fine,' I say.

Lara usually gets in at least an hour before me 'cos her college is only round the corner, so Moira feeds us both separately.

She reckons it's because we need some hot food inside us as soon as we get home but I know it's really so she can talk to each of us, on our own. Check things out. Search our eyes and faces for hidden problems.

'Had a good day?'

I nod and between mouthfuls of shepherd's pie, I tell her about the snake, spider and Soppy Sarah. Moira laughs and she looks dead proud of me when I tell her how I was chosen to demonstrate rat handling, so I don't tell her about the stuff that's bothering me. The date with Graham, that bloody newspaper, which I've got shoved down in the bottom of my bag somewhere and, of course, you! The way you've been following me round all day, making me think about the bad old days when we were kids.

Moira's dead sharp. She sees a lot. But she doesn't see you, sitting in Frank's armchair in the corner, tilting your head, grinning at me, as I get on to talking about the morning's lecture.

You sit there quietly smiling and that look on your face says it all.

'It doesn't matter what they tell you, Josie. I haven't really changed. You know that, don't you? In your mind, I'll always be the same old Alex. Wherever you go, wherever you try to hide, I'll always be with you. You'll never be free of me. I'll never let you forget what happened. What we did, Josie.'

And I know you're right. Suddenly the shepherd's pie tastes of worms and I push it away, trying not to retch.

'I'm fine!' I snap at Moira as she hovers over me. 'I'm tired that's all.'

'The water's hot,' she says. 'If you fancy a nice bath and an early night.'

37

'I'll have a quick shower,' I say. 'I'm thinking of going out.'

'Anywhere special?' she asks, trying to sound casual.

There's nothing to stop me going out. I'm a big girl. It's allowed. But generally I don't.

'New wine bar,' I mutter, making my escape.

Up in my room with a towel draped round me, I hurl clothes out of the wardrobe, trying to decide what to wear, knowing it's pointless anyway. I'm not going to go. You're not going to let me, are you, Alex?

How can I lead a normal life? How can I ever let anyone get close, with you still around? What if I freak out? Suddenly start talking to you? Talking about you? And I might. I know I might. The images are getting stronger. Taking over again. Getting me all worked up so the images get worse and it all becomes some giant bloody vicious circle.

I lie on the bed, banging my head on the pillow, watching the numbers on the digital clock change with predictable regularity. 18:35. 18:36. 18:37. While you sit there, smirking at me!

Once it gets past 19:00, I know it's too late. I'd never get to the wine bar on time now, even if I wanted to. At 19:17, I hear Frank's car pull up and I know I've been kidding myself. I could still make it if I asked Frank or Moira to give me a lift. And they would. I know they would.

You know it too, which is why you suddenly leap up. You stand on the top of my chest of drawers, wobbling a little, as if you're balancing on a ledge. Then you stand still. Your hands outstretched as if gripping onto something... slowly opening, slowly letting go.

'Don't do that,' I scream, lurching towards you, crashing into the chest of drawers as you disappear.

There's a single, sharp knock on the door and Moira's mop of curly, grey hair, with hints of the brown it used to be, appears round the door before I can even scramble to my feet.

'Are you all right?' she asks, as I try to stand up, clutching my towel with one hand, rubbing my bruised shin with the other.

'Yeah. I tripped, that's all.'

Easy enough to believe with the clothes, shoes and hairdryer littering the floor.

'I wondered whether you might like a lift into town?'

Good old Moira. I can see why they dumped me on her. She has this way of smiling at me, that makes me believe she really likes me, a softness in her voice that makes me feel good about myself.

And it's not her fault that it only lasts a second. That your voice, the other voices from my past, are stronger.

'No. No thanks,' I say. 'I've changed my mind. I'm going to have that early night.'

Maybe I even intend to. Maybe, when I flop down on the bed, I think I'll fall asleep. But I don't. I open my bedside drawer and look at the blue box. A little pressie I bought myself a few months ago, when I first started college. When everything was new and confusing. When

I wasn't sure I could cope. A pressie I never used.

I shake the box and I can hear the comforting, soft, shuffling rattle. I put it to my ear and keep shaking it for a while, letting it whisper its invitation.

It's like eating a great big gooey bar of chocolate. The best bit is staring at the bar, unwrapping it real slow. Knowing the real pleasure's still to come.

Only in this case it's not pleasure exactly. It's pain. Pain and pleasure together.

I open the box and see the sharp gleaming little points and they remind me of that time when you taught everyone to do home-made tattoos.

What a laugh that was. Out on the far corner of the playing field, under the shelter of the bushes, with the sewing needles and food dyes you nicked from the new Home Economics room that The Dragon had set up.

You did it on yourself first. Scratching out the twisting shape of a snake on your arm. Not that you were into snakes particularly but they were easy to do. Filling in the outline with dozens and dozens of needle points, dripping with colour. Making yourself bleed as you poked and prodded so that the food dyes mingled with the blood, as everyone gasped and made stupid little shrieking noises.

Everyone thought it was dead good though, when you'd finished, only no one was exactly keen to go next, were they?

So you looked around, goading and daring until Tracey stuck her arm out and screwed her eyes up tight. A flower, she wanted! Dead soppy but you did it anyway, belting her hard across the face when she started to cry as the needle dug in.

The next two 'volunteers' were too smart or too terrified to cry but Dopey David Davenport howled the place down, bringing the dinner ladies running, so you ended up in front of The Dragon again and the next morning we had one of her 'special' assemblies.

Anyone would have thought we'd been shooting up heroin out on the field, the way she went on about the dangers of sharing needles!

It was such a scream! You sat there, doubled over, cross-legged, nearly wetting yourself. All that fuss about a bit of food dye!

Dopey David's grandparents, whom he lived with, got a bit uptight and came in, ranting at The Dragon, saying you were a lunatic, a danger to other kids and why didn't she just kick you out?

Good question, I suppose. No one could understand, at the time, why you got away with so much, why The Dragon kept giving you 'second' chances. Maybe if she hadn't...maybe if you'd been sent to one of them 'special' schools, like some people said you should...then maybe, just maybe, things would have turned out differently.

But I guess she thought she was doing you a favour keeping you on. I guess she felt sorry for you. Because by that time, near the end of Year 5, your life had really gone pear-shaped, as they say, hadn't it?

Since 'Alexander the Bastard' had made his hasty departure, the day before your third birthday, your mum had never had a regular bloke. So it was just you and her, most of the time. Sure there were guys who drifted in and out but they never stayed for long. Maybe just an hour or two or overnight. Nothing that really bothered you, or so you reckoned.

If anyone ever said anything about the way your mum supplemented her benefits, you'd just thump them, wouldn't you? So people learnt to keep their mouths shut. And every time old Granny Newson sent the social services snooping round, you and your mum got rid of them pretty sharpish.

I mean the things they hinted at were disgusting, weren't they? About the strange tastes some of those blokes had. And OK, so some of the stories you told in the park and the playground about what you'd seen, what you'd done, were a bit lurid but most people reckoned you made most of them up and there was never any proof.

So you stuck together, you and your mum. Protected each other. You knew if you both kept telling the same stories, they couldn't do nothing.

Then everything changed. Your mum turned up one night with a bloke called Barry. Only he didn't drift off like the others. He stayed.

The thing you noticed first about Barry were the tattoos. He had tattoos everywhere. On his neck, up his arms, down his stomach, on his chest. Pictures of animals and army tanks. Aeroplanes, slogans, hearts, and names of girls. Dozens of girls' names.

Maybe that's where you got the idea from. Of doing the tattoos. Though why you'd want to copy him, I don't know. You hated him, right from the start, even before . . .

But I don't want to think about any of that. I don't want to remember what happened to you, how bad you got, what you did. I don't want to see it, Alex! Not again. I want to blot it all out. Forget. Make it go away.

The only thing that destroys pain is more pain. A different kind of pain.

I pick some of the little pins out of the box, running them through my fingers, letting them fall onto the bed. Then I start picking them up again. One at a time.

'Josie? What are you doing?'

It can only be Lara. Only Lara bursts in without knocking.

She stands in the doorway, her mouth slightly open, her eyes wide and confused as I cross my arms over my body, hoping she won't see. But she has.

'Moira!' she screams.

Really screams. Shrill, hysterical, jumping up and down, flapping her arms about so Moira and Frank both come bounding up the stairs.

I guess it's Frank who takes Lara away 'cos it's Moira who comes in. She doesn't say anything at first. Just picks up the pins from the bed, puts them back in the box, and seems reassured that it seems to be pretty full.

'How many?' she asks, brisk and business-like.

'Four.'

'How many?' she repeats.

'I don't know. Six, maybe seven.'

'Where?'

I hold out my left arm. Her eyes scan the scars and scratches. Old ones, mainly.

She touches a pin-shaped ridge under my skin and she flinches more than I do. Moira used to be a nurse and I know she's seen a lot in her time but this seems to freak her.

'Get dressed,' she says. 'I'll take you to A&E.'

I shake my head, cursing myself as the tears start to come.

A&E means doctors, forms to be filled in, reports to be filed. It means trouble.

'Can't you do it?' I ask, pleading.

She shakes her head but she's wavering. She knows what it might mean for me, if it gets out. What I've done to myself. Again.

Chapter 5

Moira did the job herself. I knew she didn't want to. I knew she'd be in big trouble if anything went wrong. If my arm went septic. If anyone found out.

So I knew she'd taken a big risk for me and I didn't argue when she told me I had to stay home on Thursday and Friday.

I don't like missing college but I knew Moira wanted to keep an eye on me, keep dressing the wounds, making sure I didn't do any more.

She wanted to talk, too. And, believe me, that sort of digging is worse than having those pins dug out of my flesh. But I felt like I owed her something and besides, talking to her was better than talking to you all the time.

And I knew it wouldn't make any difference to anything, to the way Moira thinks about me, 'cos she already knows the full story. One of the few who needed to know.

So I told her what it was like after Barry moved in with your mum. How you went completely loopy. How you just got worse and worse. But when she asked me why, I couldn't really answer her. It was a bit of a mystery. Nobody really knew. And if you did, you never let on.

On the surface, to outsiders, Barry seemed OK. A bit loud, a bit prone to throwing his fists around when he'd had a bit too much to drink, which was most Friday and Saturday nights. But he didn't go out during the week and he had a steady job, which was more than could be said for a lot of the blokes round our way. He was a self-employed plumber and had just bought himself a big, new, white van, when he met your mum.

You were never quite sure where or how they met and maybe that was part of the problem. Barry wasn't from the estate and he never said a word about where he'd lived before or anything about his background or family, like he was hiding something. Too right, as it turned out!

Old Granny Newson liked him. Acted quite flirty with him sometimes, the demented old bat!

'Oooh, Barry, you couldn't just pop in for a minute, could you? I think I've got a blockage in my U-bend.'

He never charged her. Or any of the other neighbours.

'Regular bloody knight in shining overalls,' you used to say.

The neighbours thought so and the whisper went round that he was a lucky catch. Far too good for your mum.

Trouble was, he wasn't happy playing the perfect plumber or the perfect partner, he wanted to play the perfect step-dad too.

So, maybe that was it, as I told Moira. You didn't want a step-dad telling you what to do. When you could go out, what you could and couldn't wear, when you had to be in. Getting your mum on his side all the time, turning her against you. Your mum had always been dead easy-going but Barry was different. Always throwing his weight around. Literally sometimes.

'What with him at home and The Dragon at school, I may as well be in bloody prison,' you used to say.

'Was it really that bad?' Moira asked.

'I don't know, do I? All I'm saying is that's how it seemed to Alex, at the time.'

And I knew, as I said it, that it sounded feeble. Lots of kids hate their step-parents. Plenty of them hate their real parents. But they don't all flip over the edge, do they? Even when they realize the person in question's an even bigger lying, cheating shit than they thought.

You found out the truth about Barry that last Wednesday afternoon of the summer holidays before we started back in Year 6. You needed some new trousers and shoes for school, so you were going shopping with your mum. Just you and her, it was supposed to be, but then he turned up at lunchtime.

'I'm working over that way this afternoon,' Barry said. 'I'll give you a lift. Save you getting the bus. I can pick you up on the way back as well, if you like.'

You didn't like, of course, but when you told him where he could stick his lift, your mum just belted you over the head and told you not to be so rude. She told you off for sulking and banging your feet in the back of the van too, so by the time you reached the shopping centre, you were well cheesed off. Cheese that turned decidedly mouldy when Barry announced he had half an hour to spare and might as well pop into the centre with you for a bit.

'So there we were, playing happy families,' you said when you told the story later.

Everyone was under the slide at the time, smoking the ciggies you'd managed to nick on your shopping trip. Everyone was trying not to cough, 'cos we were all trying to pretend that we smoked all the time. Besides everyone could see by the look in your eyes that it was going to be some story.

'Him and Mum strolling along, holding hands,' you said, pulling a face as you spoke. 'Him nibbling at her ear every so often and me hanging behind them trying not to puke . . . when someone calls his name and we all turn round . . . well, there's plenty of blokes in the world called Barry and, for a second, he tried to make out it wasn't him the woman was shouting at. But she came rushing over, swinging a carrier bag round and round before smashing it into Barry's stomach. I don't know what was in the bag but it must have been something pretty heavy, 'cos he doubled up and had to let go of my mum's hand.'

You grinned as you said that and lit another cigarette. No one spoke. No one asked who the woman was. It was too obvious, I guess. Most had witnessed scenes like that, if only on telly.

'His wife had nearly as many tattoos as he had,' you said. 'And she's yelling and swearing and Barry looks like he's going to thump her or summat. But he doesn't 'cos by then there's a big crowd gathering around tutting. And it's obvious they're all going to be on her side 'cos it's like mainly oldies or women with kids, who look like they've

48

been dumped too. So they all start nodding, sympathetic like, when she starts screaming about the maintenance he hasn't paid and how the kids keep asking why their dad hasn't been to see 'em for months and months...'

You paused then, realizing you'd missed an important bit out of your story. You were never much good at stories. Never quite got the hang of a beginning, a middle and an end, did you?

'She had the kids with her,' you said, filling in the gap. 'And the whole lot of 'em looked as though they belonged to a circus or summat. Weird or what? There's her with her tattoos, long, flowery skirt and flip flops. Then there's a girl, who looks about fifteen, with a really white face, black lips, loads of black stuff round her eyes and a spiky collar round her neck. She's dead tall and thin. Very thin. Wearing a black strappy T-shirt with a purple bra underneath. Don't know why she needed a bra. She had no boobs and you could see her shoulder blades, sticking up all sharp and pointy, like her miserable face.'

You paused again when you said that, nudged Tracey out of the way, and sat down on the damp grass under the slide.

'There was another girl, about eight, I reckon. All sort of small and red and dumpy, like a squashed tomato so the two of 'em didn't look nothing like sisters at all. And the squashed tomato had these great dribbly tears running down her blotchy face, looking dead pathetic and stupid. But the little one was the worst. Podgy little girl with blonde curly hair, like a floppy rag doll or summat. And

49

while all the yelling and swearing's going on, she's running round in circles screaming "booble, booble, poop, poop" or summat daft like that . . .'

You'd got it all wrong, of course.

The eldest girl was only twelve, The Tomato was ten and the little mad one wasn't even a girl at all. That was three-year-old Denzil.

You got it all sorted out though, soon enough. Barry's wife saw to that. Once she'd got him cornered, she wasn't going to let him go so easy. Oh, no. She'd had enough of his 'pissing about', she said. She didn't care what he was doing or what sort of tart he was living with. He could rot in hell, for all she cared but he was going to pay up or she'd have the law onto him. And, what's more, he was going to take the 'bloody kids' off her hands once in a while.

Once in a while turned out to be every weekend. And that would have suited you fine, if he'd buzzed off home to see 'em, leaving you and your mum in peace. But that's not what his wife had in mind at all.

So every weekend from then on you got the 'the freak show', as you took to calling it.

'It'll be lovely, Alex,' your mum tried to tell you, that first time. 'Thalia's your age. I thought she could share—'

'No way!' you yelled. 'What do you think I am? I'm not having some scabby-faced girl sharing anything of mine. I'm not having any of 'em anywhere near me.'

You had to though 'cos it wasn't a big house. So you ended up having to share your telly, your games machine, your bike . . . not to mention sharing your mum and sharing your bedroom with little Denzil. Crazy people. Crazy names. The eldest was Odette but you called her Oddball.

And, after that first weekend, your mum stopped telling you, 'It'll be lovely,' because, clearly, it wasn't going to be.

Oddball and her dad spent the whole time yelling and swearing at each other, mainly over the fact that she wouldn't eat. You didn't care about that. You didn't care whether she ate or not and they could snarl at each other as much as they liked. But when Oddball started on your mum, that was different.

'Eat more?' she screamed, at one point. 'So I end up like that fat tart over there! Get real!'

You tried to go for her but you fell over Denzil who was crawling about on all fours, barking and drooling like a rabid dog.

'You'd like some chips, wouldn't you, Thalia?' your mum asked.

The Tomato looked at Oddball, but Oddball just shrugged so Thalia took the chips, shovelling them into her scabby mouth, not saying a word.

The Tomato never spoke. Well, hardly ever. There was no reason she shouldn't. No medical reason, anyway. She was an 'elective mute', to give it its fancy name. Which basically means she didn't speak because she didn't want to.

That wasn't her only problem either. She had psoriasis, which is why she was so red and blotchy. So maybe you should have felt just a little bit sorry for her instead of

51

calling her 'Scabby', 'Spot' and 'Tomato Face'. But 'empathy', understanding how others felt, was never your strong suit, was it?

You didn't care how they felt. You just wanted the whole lot of them out of your life. Barry and his tattoos, Oddball and her eating disorder, Thalia with her flaky skin and Denzil with his bed wetting and stupid noises.

Your mum tried harder than you did, at least for a while. Putting up with all the crap from Oddball, trying to get The Tomato to talk, picking up Denzil, trying to cuddle him, trying not to mind when she got a foot in her stomach or a fist in her eye. Not that Denzil was violent. He didn't mean to kick and stuff. It was just that he was so hyperactive. He couldn't handle being cuddled or anything that involved being still.

It used to really make you mad, seeing your mum running around after them all, trying to be nice, trying to please them. Even worse was when she stopped trying, when she realized it was pointless. When you'd hear her on Saturday mornings, in the bedroom, crying, after Barry went to pick them up. When you'd see her swigging vodka and taking tablets by the dozen just to get her through the weekend.

You'd want to go out. Want to stay in. You didn't know what you wanted. And, if you did manage to get out, Denzil would never be far behind. He liked you, Alex. I don't know why. Probably because he was barking mad. And maybe there was part of you that sort of liked him too. 'Cos I reckon Denzil made you feel a bit special, didn't he? The way he followed you around...

I stopped then, partly because I felt sick and partly because Moira was looking at me all sort of funny and I realized that I hadn't been talking to her. I'd been talking to you again.

'And how do you feel?' Moira asked. 'When you think about—'

'I don't know, do I?' I yelled. 'What's it got to do with me? This is Alex's story. This isn't about me. How am I supposed to think about me with all this other shit still in my head? This is Alex I'm telling you about. Alex! It's always bloody Alex. It's all I can ever think about. What happened back then. But you already know that, don't you? So what's the bloody point?'

Moira looked like she was going to say something else but she didn't 'cos Lara had wandered in from the kitchen with a bag of bread rolls in her hand.

So it must have been Thursday afternoon, when we had that particular conversation, because that's Lara's afternoon off, when she doesn't have to go in to her college.

'Not those, Lara,' Moira said, looking at the bread rolls. 'Those are the new ones I got this morning. The old stuff is on the top of the bread bin.'

'Top of the bread bin,' Lara repeated, as if it was a piece of really new and exciting information.

It wasn't. Moira always left the stuff for the ducks on top of the bread bin. It's one of Lara's little rituals to go down to the park and feed the ducks. It's a proper park not like the dog-poo covered green we played on when

53

we were kids. It's got tennis courts, a putting green, a proper fenced off kiddies' play area, a café and a boating lake.

Not that I ever go but Lara loves it.

'Only half an hour, mind,' Moira said. 'It's getting dark.'

'Half an hour,' Lara repeated.

She came and gave me a hug before she left and I tried not to wince, tried not to pull away. It wasn't anything to do with Lara. It's just that sometimes I don't feel like hugs, don't want anyone to touch me, and besides she was pressing on my arm, where Moira had pulled those pins out.

Chapter 6

Usually it helps, talking to Moira. But, somehow, it hasn't this time. She knows it too, which is why she wasn't keen to go to church this morning.

She and Frank go most Sundays and take Lara with them. It's one of those happy clappy places. I went once, just to see what it was like. Drove me nuts. All those people hugging and smiling and arm waving, thanking Jesus for taking away their sins.

Sins? What did any of them know about sins when probably the worst thing they'd ever done was park on a double yellow line?

'I'll be fine,' I told Moira, as Lara clutched eagerly at her arm. 'I won't do anything daft. I promise.'

They went but I know they'll come straight back after the service. They won't stay for coffee. Moira knows, as much as I do, that my promises don't always mean much.

She left me settled at the computer with my college work. We've all had to choose an animal rights issue to discuss. Sarah's doing factory farming and I know she'll get top marks. She always does on theory. Graham chose the use of animal organs in transplants. That's the one I fancied really but, by the time I'd got around to choosing, three others had already picked it, so I ended up with cosmetic testing.

I think I've done it pretty well. Put both sides of the argument, so now I've only got the conclusion to do. Sum up. Give my own opinion. Well, that's easy enough. Bunch of sadistic scientists hell bent on making money for greedy cosmetic companies who prey on pathetic human vanity.

Or is that too simplistic? Too right, it is. So do it properly, Josie. Take your time.

That's the trouble with this thinking business. I don't see things clearly anymore in black and white. It's all issues dressed up in fuzzy shades of grey and politically correct jargon. I could sit here for hours being reasonable!

Sometimes I think it was simpler when we were kids. When we trod on beetles in the playground just to hear them go crunch. When we threw stones at animals in the street just for target practice. Or even at people, if they were smaller and slower than us. Little kids and wrinklies, mainly.

We didn't think much about what we said either.

'Do that again and I'll kick your head in,' was about the nearest we ever got to reasoning.

'I'll bloody kill you,' was a common threat.

Which is why no one thought much about it when you started mouthing off that Monday, just before the Christmas holiday.

Why does every single thought I have lead back to you? How can I start off thinking about cosmetic testing and end up thinking about you and your loud mouth? I'm not even thinking about it, as such. Your voice is actually there, yelling inside my head, setting off that pain above my right eye again.

'I'll kill 'em, I will,' you shouted, so the whole flaming school could hear. 'I swear I'll shoot the whole bloody lot of 'em.'

No prizes for guessing who you were talking about. It had been a bad weekend. Nobody really knew why. You didn't go into details. But as you'd thrown a chair at Dopey David and stabbed Amrit with a compass even before register was over, it was fairly obvious you weren't in a good mood.

We had Mr Khan in Year 6, who always knew what to do. He asked Mrs Bell, one of the class 'helpers' to take you out for a bit, till you'd calmed down. A 'bit' turned out to be half the morning but after break you were considered safe enough to be allowed to join the Christmas Panto dress rehearsal. Bad, bad decision.

The Christmas Show was The Dragon's idea, of course. Infants were doing a Nativity, Years 3 and 4 were doing poems and songs and the two top years were lumbered with the pantomime. All of which were going to be performed to parents on Tuesday evening and then again on Wednesday afternoon, just before we broke up.

Two performances. Would you believe that? The Dragon had managed to sell enough tickets, at a pound each, to fill the hall twice over. Another sign of how she was starting to turn the school around. Getting parents involved. Getting them in to watch their little dears perform.

Not that it looked as though there was going to be a performance, at that point. Everyone was so hyped up in their wigs and make-up that they'd forgotten a few of the basics, like where to stand and what to say.

'All right, Cinders,' The Dragon told Tracey. 'You're in the kitchen, peeling potatoes, when the ugly sisters come in, remember? And, Alex, you tell her to get on with it and ask her why she hasn't swept the floor.'

You stood there in that daft purple wig and huge painted lips, glaring at The Dragon. You'd told her you didn't want to be in no stupid pantomime right at the beginning.

'Oh but we're *all* going to be in it,' she'd informed you. 'And you know what, Alex? I've got a big part in mind for you because I think you could be a real little star. You've got a natural comic talent, hidden away in there, you know.'

'Silly cow,' you'd muttered but I reckon you were sort of pleased, deep down 'cos you'd learnt most of your lines and had been really throwing yourself into it.

Only on the day of the dress rehearsal, I guess you weren't feeling in much of a funny mood. And anyone who really knew you would have been able to tell that you weren't even in that hall at all. You were back at home seeing Denzil peeing on your football shirt, when he decided to use the bottom of your wardrobe as a toilet. Watching Barry smash your skateboard to pieces against the garden wall because you wouldn't let his precious Tomato have a go on it. Seeing Oddball spitting food at your mum like a bulimic cobra.

58

'Wake up Alex!' The Dragon prompted. 'Why haven't you swept...'

'Why haven't you swept the floor, Cinders?' you mumbled. 'And what are you peeling bloody potatoes for? 'Cos I'm not gonna eat 'em, am I? They're full of calories, aren't they? You stupid, fat bitch!'

'Alex!' said The Dragon, as everyone started whooping and laughing. 'I don't mind a bit of improvisation here and there but I don't think the ugly step-sister would say that.'

'She would,' you insisted. ''Cos mine does.'

'Yes,' said The Dragon, silencing everyone with one of her stares. 'Well, I suppose all families are different. But our little play's about Cinderella's family and—'

'Stuff Cinderella's family!' you said, suddenly pulling off your wig and throwing it at The Dragon. 'She ought to have mine to put up with, then she'd bloody know, wouldn't she? It'd take more than a Fairy-bloody-Godmother to sort them out. It'd need a bloody machine gun.'

You'd lost it by then. Completely lost it. Arms flailing about, knocking over props and scenery. The pans fell off their hooks, the backcloth collapsed and the pumpkin sailed across the stage, smashing into orange pulp at The Dragon's feet. It took her and two other teachers a good ten minutes to restrain you and, naturally, it was the end of your acting career. The third white mouse got a sudden promotion to ugly sister and you were excluded for the last two days of term.

You were still yelling and swearing when your mum came to take you home, blaming everyone but yourself as usual.

'I didn't do nothing! It's not fair!'

And I guess you really believed it. In your mind it was The Dragon's fault, your mum's fault, anybody's fault. Everybody's fault but yours.

Barry saw it differently, of course. Locked you in your room till you apologized. Not so much for what had happened at school but because you'd kicked, punched and spat at your mum on the way home.

You were still locked in your room on Christmas morning, screaming that you didn't care what he did to you. You didn't care if you died in there.

It was all a bit of an act, really, the screaming. You were quite happy in there for a few days, I reckon, watching videos, eating the sweets your mum slipped into you and dropping notes out of the window to your mates. Telling them you were being held hostage. Asking them to send ransom money. Some of the daft eejits did as well! You made almost ten quid and you thought it was well funny.

But being locked up on Christmas morning was different. Not funny at all. So you raised the stakes a bit. Started yelling about the stuff Barry had already done to you. Lies, most people reckoned, but they couldn't be sure, could they? And Granny Newson's bony fingers must have been reaching for that phone, wondering whether she could reach social services on Christmas Day.

Only then it all sort of went quiet and by the afternoon you were out on the street with the new skateboard your mum had bought you.

'Well, I had to say sorry, didn't I?' you told people. 'Or Barry would have given my new skateboard to Scabby Chops when she comes tomorrow.'

True enough but it wasn't the real reason you'd backed down, was it? Oh no! The truth was that you'd had an idea. A way to get your own back.

Later you claimed you'd got the idea from a video you'd been watching – 'Christmas Day Massacre'. Only you called your version 'Boxing Day Surprise'.

It was a surprise too. Only it shouldn't have been, should it? 'Cos the clues were all there, especially when you went beetling off to Connor's later that afternoon.

Absolute head-case, Connor Lyecroft was. Lived two streets away. You couldn't miss him. Always wore combat gear and a black balaclava, even in summer.

Couldn't wait to join the army when he left school. Only they wouldn't have him, would they? He reckoned it was because he failed the eye test. Reckoned he was colour blind or something. But he wasn't. There was nothing wrong with his eyes. Just his head.

He was dead thick. Probably failed all the tests. He didn't let it put him off though. He still stalked round the estate in his balaclava, like he was the flaming SAS or something, taking pot shots at anything that moved, with his air rifle.

That probably explains why I don't ever remember

seeing many birds round our way. And I don't reckon the local cats were much safer. Granny Newson swore it was Connor who 'did for her little Ginger'.

We all knew Connor was a head-case but he was a bit of a hero too, to us kids. You could always rely on Connor to pop in the off-licence and buy ciggies and cans of lager. He'd supply other stuff too. Knives, weed, cheap CDs and games machines. There was nothing Connor couldn't get his hands on, for a price. And the price wasn't always money, if you know what I mean.

You never let on how you managed to get stuff from Connor, did you, Alex? All people knew was that you could wheedle almost anything out of him, even one of his prize possessions.

You made sure it was dark before you came back. And late enough for your mum and Barry to be too pissed to notice what you were sneaking into the house. You even phoned half a dozen of your mates to tell them to be watching.

'Eleven o'clock tomorrow morning,' you said. 'Never mind what! Wait and see. It'll be a laugh.'

It didn't quite work to plan though, 'cos Barry had one heck of a hangover and probably wouldn't have got out of bed at all if you hadn't woken him.

Seconds later his wife was on the phone screaming her own reminder that he was supposed to 'pick up the bloody kids' and at five past eleven, the little audience saw him staggering out, zipping up his trousers, before falling into his van and screeching off down the street.

'Man drives off in van' was a bit of an anti-climax but a note appeared at your window.

'Wait and see.'

Everyone hung around, waiting for forty minutes or more, till the van screeched back up the street and something else appeared at your now-open window.

'Shit!' Tracey screamed. 'It's a bloody machine gun!'

By then it was too late. Oddball was stretching her skeletal legs out of the passenger seat and The Tomato was scrambling out of the back with a squirming, kicking Denzil in her arms when you fired.

Most people dropped to the ground, screaming, so they didn't even see The Tomato drop Denzil, or Oddball clutching her chest as a patch of red spread across her white jumper. They didn't see Barry look up at the window as your next shot hit him full in the face.

Some of them must have heard you laughing though, above the sound of their own screams. Must have dared raise their eyes, because suddenly they're laughing too.

It took others longer to catch on. To realize that although Oddball was screaming, shaking and grasping her flat chest with gory, red hands, she was still standing. That Barry was managing a whole lot of cursing and yelling for a man who'd just been shot in the face and that the red stuff Denzil was happily licking off his trousers wasn't blood at all.

'It's paint!' Liam screeched. 'It was a paintball gun! Bloody brilliant!'

You bounced down the stairs, pushed past your mum,

who was standing looking bemused in the doorway and darted out onto the street. You might have missed your chance in the panto but there you were, centre stage, centre of attention, all eyes on you. Including Barry's red, stinging eyes.

Somehow you'd miscalculated, though. Probably thought everyone would see it how you saw it, as a bit of a laugh, a harmless prank. That Barry wouldn't go for you, out in the street, with everyone watching.

But he did. Grabbed hold of you, slammed you up against the side of the van, bashing your head against the metal, over and over.

'Stop it!' your mum screamed, trying to drag Barry away.

'It was only paint!' you cried out.

'Only paint!' he yelled throwing you to the ground. 'What about Thalia's skin and what about my eyes? You could have blinded me, you stupid—'

His foot lashed out as he swore but he stopped himself mid kick 'cos little Denzil had hurled himself on top of you.

I don't know whether Denzil was just being loopy or whether he did it to protect you ... and I don't want to think about it. I don't want to think about it anymore.

'I said I don't want to think about YOU anymore! So it's no good lying there on the floor, Alex, trying to make me remember. Trying to make me feel sorry for you! Because it doesn't change anything, does it? It doesn't excuse what you did! And I won't look. I'm closing my eyes, see?'

But it doesn't make any difference. Eyes shut. Eyes open. I can still see you lying there, by the van, with blood, real blood, streaming from your nose. Dripping into your mouth. Turning you into the victim, that time.

Your mum hugging you, your mates gathering round you later. Telling you what a laugh you were, what a humourless, nasty shit Barry was.

Your mum even talked about dumping Barry. And maybe if she had ... maybe ...

'Away in a manger, no crib for a bed,

The little Lord Jesus laid down his sweet head.'

They're back already. Lara's voice reminds me that it's only a couple of weeks off Christmas in real time too and stops me going down the 'maybe, if only' route to nowhere again. Seconds later Lara's in the room, throwing her arms round me.

'Jesus saves sinners,' she announces gleefully, her smiling face about a centimetre away from mine.

Well, I'm not sure about that but for your sake and mine, Alex, I can't help hoping she's right.

Chapter 7

Like I said, I don't know about Jesus but Lara sure saves my sanity sometimes. What's left of it. Moira just smiles and says it's Jesus working through Lara. But that's all she says. She never tries to ram her religion down my throat.

'Can we do hairdressers today?' Lara asked, as soon as she'd finished carol singing.

It's one of Lara's favourite Sunday afternoon 'games', is hairdressers. I didn't really feel like it, but I knew she'd be hurt if I refused so I got all the stuff ready... shampoo, hairdryer and 'Mahogany' toner because Lara's decided she wants her light brown hair to be dark, like mine.

It doesn't turn out to be anything like as dark as mine but I trim the split ends, rub a bit of gel through and blow dry it, while we watch the football with Frank. I get a bit excited when United score and bash Lara over the head with the hairdryer but she forgives me. She leaps up, stares at herself in the mirror over the fireplace and I can tell she's dead pleased.

Moira's pleased too. Sees our cosy family afternoon as a sign that I'm 'coming round' and safe to go back to college.

Unfortunately I don't go straight to college on a Monday because my first seminar's not till eleven. So at half past nine I have an hour-long session with my social worker. 'A little chat', as she likes to call them.

It's harmless enough today, I suppose. All about how I'm getting on at college. Nothing deep. Nothing about the past. Nothing about you. Or what we did. And it's not her fault that I find it hard to open up. I just don't like social workers. Stems from the couple of times I was taken into care as a kid, I suppose.

Anyway I tell her what I'm going to tell Graham. That I missed Thursday and Friday because I had a cold. And if Moira wants to tell her something different, well, that's up to Moira, isn't it?

Maybe stomach bug would be better than a cold when I tell Graham. 'Cos you wouldn't stand someone up for a cold, would you? But you'd have to if you were stuck in the loo puking up, wouldn't you?

On the other hand, is that a picture of me I want him to have? Vomiting into the lav? Oh, I don't know. I'll sort something out. I won't see him till this afternoon anyway. He's not in my first class 'cos he does a different module.

I knew it was a mistake, eating at college. I only took the chance 'cos my tutor kept me late and I didn't think I'd have time to nip into town and get back for the two o'clock lecture.

It was packed in the snack bar so I grabbed a tray and joined the massive queue. Only I never got to eat anything because just as my hand was about to reach out to grab a cheese and tomato roll, I heard the shrieking laugh. Sounded like a hyena on speed, so it just had to be Soppy Sarah.

Head thrown back, so her blonde hair flicks into the face of her companion. But he doesn't mind. Oh no. Graham's laughing too as he picks up a serviette and wipes the big blob of cream, which had caused all the fuss, from the end of his nose.

Well, OK, a couple of students having a laugh together. But as Graham puts the serviette down, his arm slips round the back of Sarah's shoulders. He pats her back because she's laughing so much, she's about to choke. And I wish she would! Because when all the laughing and patting's finished, Graham's arm stays put and he leans forward to whisper something to her so his lips are almost touching her cheek . . .

''Scuse me!'

The people behind have got a bit agitated and start pushing past me. And I don't know whether to keep moving forward or try to barge my way out. Have Sarah and Graham seen me? Do they care? Does it matter? Do I care?

It's not as though me and Graham were going out or anything, I tell myself as I finally decide to bolt for the door. I didn't even make the first date, did I? So there's no reason he and Sarah shouldn't be sitting there stuffing their faces with cream buns. No reason he shouldn't have his arm round her. Maybe it doesn't even mean anything. Maybe.

It's raining outside so I head straight for the lecture

hall, flopping into a seat at the back, hoping the cold, silent air and the couple of paracetamol I swallow will calm the fire that's raging in my head. That's what it's like. Fire. The flames shooting up behind my eyes, the hissing and crackling in my ears and the thick, black smoke suffocating me, inside.

The lecture theatre's empty, so when I see a figure materialize through smoke and dancing flames, I know who it is.

'Go away! I don't want you here. Not now.'

But you're there. Looking exactly as you did on the first day of your trial, when your defence team had dressed you up all nice and neat with the blue shirt that reflected your enormous blue eyes and your short, blonde hair brushed and shiny.

You actually raised a gasp when you appeared in court. How could someone who looked like that be responsible for so much carnage?

'This is nothing to do with you!' I hear myself shouting out, my voice echoing round the hall, bouncing back at me. 'This is me. My life. My problem. Go away!'

'Josie? Josie, are you OK?'

The angelic figure starts to fade, slowly taking on another form. Still small. Still wearing a blue shirt but with a bushy ginger beard and gold rimmed specs.

'You were shouting out,' Mr Phinn says.

'Er…I came in early. Must have nodded off,' I say.

He puts his briefcase down, sits in the seat in front of me and leans over, staring.

'You look a bit flushed,' he says, examining my face as if for signs of illegal substance abuse.

'Time of the month,' I say.

You can tell just by looking at Mr Phinn that he's the type to be embarrassed by 'women's problems'. And sure enough he leaps out of his seat, like he's just discovered he's been sitting on a porcupine or something, grabs his bag and beetles off down to the front, muttering apologies.

He potters about, getting his lecture notes ready and I know he wouldn't try to stop me if I just got up and walked out. But people are already starting to drift in and besides the tablets have kicked in and I feel a bit better now. I think.

Even when Sarah and Graham stroll in, holding hands, I can handle it. What did I expect? I'd stood him up, hadn't I? Besides, it wouldn't have worked. I'm not stupid. I knew that. I'm not ready. Maybe Graham sensed I wasn't that keen. Like Moira says, best just to concentrate on my work.

Easy enough with Mr Phinn. He might look like a bit of a jerk but he's a good lecturer.

'What,' he booms at us, as pictures start to flash up on the screen, 'is the most dangerous animal on earth?'

We're not meant to answer. Just watch the pictures and think.

'The Great White Shark?' he asks. 'The African elephant? The small but deadly Black Widow spider? Crocodiles? Tigers? Rhinos? You wouldn't want one of

70

them charging at you at fifty miles an hour, would you? Or what about these?'

The picture changes to show a ridiculously happy family enjoying the sort of picnic you see on adverts for margarine. Wicker hamper, red and white check cloth spread out on short green grass. And not a wasp in sight.

Another picture shows the debris after they've left and we begin to get the idea.

'Two minutes,' Mr Phinn tells us, 'to jot down all the potential dangers to animals and the environment.'

Sarah, who's sitting a few rows in front of me, starts scribbling even before he's finished speaking. I haven't even got my note pad out!

Won't matter if I don't get it all down though, 'cos it's pretty obvious stuff and I'll remember the main points for when I get home.

Besides, he's going through it all now. Step by step, in graphic detail. A hedgehog's got stuck in the plastic holder that bound their four cans of Coke together. Sheep are wandering out onto the road through the gate they've left open. A swan has fallen victim to one of Dad's fishing hooks. And, all the while, the little fire they've left burning is scorching the grass, as they roar off in their car.

'Man!' Mr Phinn snarls. 'A danger to animals, to the environment and ultimately—'

Graham's dropped his pen and I think he touches Sarah's leg, as he bends to pick it up because she gives a stupid little squeal.

71

'And ultimately,' Mr Phinn repeats, glaring at Sarah, 'man becomes a danger to himself.'

Well, he's laying it on a bit thick, of course. And it's unlikely that just one family could cause all that chaos with their picnic. Or is it? Doesn't it only need one crazy person, one thoughtless action...?

And suddenly, there's a picture of you on the screen. You standing on that bridge.

How could Mr Phinn have got that picture? Why is he doing this to me? What does he know?

It takes me a second to realize. Just in time to stop myself shouting out.

It's not Mr Phinn's picture. He's switched off the machine. It's my picture. In my head again. But it doesn't make it any less real. And no matter how much I blink and rub my eyes, it won't go away.

I can see that bridge as clearly as on the day it was opened.

There'd been a right fuss to get it built in the first place. Some idiot had thought it was a good idea to widen the road which ran through the middle of our estate. Link it up with the new section of motorway. Make access to the new out-of-town shopping centre easier. The work took years, of course. Caused absolute chaos while it was going on. And even more chaos when it was finished.

How they ever got those plans passed, I don't know. There were hints of dubious dealing, of money changing hands. I even think a couple of people were prosecuted

72

later. There must have been some sort of dodgy dealing involved because the whole business was ridiculous.

They said the new road was supposed to make it easier for estate residents, so they didn't feel so out on a limb, so isolated. So they could go and spend all the money they didn't have in the new shopping centre, I suppose.

Well, sure, they could do that. And sure it was quicker to get to the motorway. Which is why all the lorry drivers took to using it. But it had chopped our estate in half, hadn't it? Us on one side and our primary school on the other, for a start. With not so much as a flaming zebra crossing, would you believe? Roundabout at the top and traffic lights about a mile down, but what use were they? We weren't going to walk a mile out of our way just to cross a road, were we? So we took our chances, darting between the buses and the lorries.

Maybe the councillors, or whatever prats make these decisions, thought local parents weren't the sort to fuss if a few of their kids got splattered. But they were wrong. My mum didn't do nothing but there were plenty around who did. Got up a petition, wrote letters, made phone calls and, when that didn't work, organized a demonstration, blocking the new road with their cars.

Another set of lights was hastily put up but that wasn't good enough. By then, locals had got the scent of real victory and demanded an underpass or a pedestrian bridge.

There was a right stink. The road had to be closed again, while the work took place. They decided against an underpass, allegedly because an underpass would be an open invitation to muggers, druggies and vagrants. But I reckon it was because they didn't fancy tunnelling under their nice, new road. A bridge would be cheaper, quicker, safer.

Well, yes, I suppose it would have been safer if they'd built it properly. Made it child-proof, vandal-proof. But I don't expect the designers had kids of their own. 'Cos if they had, they'd have known, wouldn't they? They'd have spotted what we spotted when we first trotted across it, at the start of the spring term in Year 6.

It had metal railings, not solid brick sides. Nice metal railings that you could shove things through, down onto the busy road below.

Why should we want to? I ask myself now. Because we could, I suppose. Because it was fun watching crisp packets and sweet wrappers floating down like coloured leaves. It was a laugh hearing the tinny clink of Coke cans, bouncing off the cars. We didn't think how the drivers might be distracted. Or maybe we just didn't care.

There was another problem with the bridge too. One that some of the sharper parents picked up on straight away. The thick metal bar which ran across the top of the railings was only about head height to the average kid and it wasn't long before we started putting our hands on the bar, pulling ourselves up and leaning over.

It was safe enough. We weren't stupid enough to lean too far. To topple over. But that's what some of the parents feared, which is why they started another campaign to have the rails raised and put closer together.

I reckon it was people bleating about the dangers which got you started.

'Now I don't want anyone being silly on that bridge,' The Dragon said, one morning in assembly.

At least part of her message must have stuck in your head. The words 'silly' and 'bridge', because that night, on the way home, you started being silly, big time.

Coke cans weren't good enough for you, were they? You had to start dropping stones, didn't you? Small ones, at first. Then bigger ones.

'Dangerous, dangerous behaviour,' Mr Phinn's voice shouts out. 'But we never learn, do we?'

Haven't a clue what he's on about. I've completely lost track. Like I always used to do at school. Trying to listen, trying to pay attention but somehow finding myself somewhere else entirely.

My concentration's usually pretty good these days but not now. Not this afternoon.

I'm trying to work out whether you knew what you were doing. Whether you actually planned to do what you did that Saturday morning in early February or whether you just took your chance when you saw Barry's van.

'Playing' on that bridge had got to be our favourite game. Sitting on the floor, with our feet dangling through the rails, or hanging over the top, knowing it would get

75

a reaction from passing adults. Sometimes the added bonus of drivers looking up in panic, wondering what we were going to drop.

Something had got to you that morning. Probably something your mum had done. Or something Barry had said, as he'd stormed off to pick up his freaky kids. Just the fact that they were about to descend would have been enough to set you off, I guess.

I know you said you'd found that huge lump of brick. But was it as simple as that? Would you have 'found' it if you hadn't been looking?

'Looking for mischief', as Granny Newson used to say, whenever she saw you lurking around.

It was one of those times when you got everyone wound up, the half dozen kids who were there with you not quite knowing what was going on in your head or even in their own.

Big chunks of brick dropped onto roads were dangerous. Really dangerous. We all knew that. Even you knew that. Which is why people were pretty confident you weren't actually going to do it.

You were just mucking about, weren't you? Standing on tiptoe, holding the brick, balanced on top of the rail. Hastily dragging it back and shoving it up your jacket when the hiss went round that someone was coming, which wasn't as often as you'd think, 'cos not many people used that bridge at weekends. They were all in bed or out in their cars, I guess.

Besides, it was raining that day. Just a bit of misty

drizzle, I seem to remember, but enough to stop most people going walkabout.

'Go on, Alex,' Liam giggled, as you struck up your pose again. 'Go on, drop it. I dare you.'

Dare. Dangerous word that.

Your arms dropped. Everyone gasped or screamed.

But you'd held onto the brick. That time.

Chapter 8

You knew, didn't you, Alex? You knew how stupid it was. Everyone knew. But it was just too tempting, wasn't it? When you saw Barry's van.

Not difficult to spot. White, with his name painted in red on the sides and again on the great lump of plastic piping he had fixed to the top.

Was it co-incidence that he drove past when you had that brick in your hand? Or had you planned it? You knew he'd drive past that way, didn't you? But had you really planned to drop that brick or did you do it on impulse? Were you trying to kill him? Scare him? What were you thinking, Alex? Were you even thinking at all? Or was your mind just one big, black, venomous cloud of mixed-up emotions as usual?

Whatever. I don't know. But if you'd planned to get back at Barry, it didn't work out, did it? 'Cos your grasp of maths and physics was a bit dodgy, like your grasp of most things. Barry's van had already reached the bridge as you let go of the brick. Had already passed safely under as the brick fell, crashing to the ground right in front of that blue Fiesta.

Everyone scattered pretty sharpish, so we never found out if the front wheel actually hit the brick or whether the driver, an elderly lady, simply panicked and swerved.

We didn't look back when we heard the crash and it was only later we found out that she'd hit a Rover, coming the other way, head on.

The cars were both write-offs, the local news bulletin said. But the drivers and the two little kiddies in the back of the Rover were fine. Not a scratch on any of them. They were lucky.

YOU were lucky.

No one split, of course. Too scared? Too guilty? Too stupid?

Whatever. No one cracked. Not when parents asked. Not when the cops came snooping round. Not even when The Dragon glared down at us in Monday's assembly.

'If any of you,' she said, 'know anything about this terrible act of mindless vandalism, then you must come and tell me.'

No chance. Though it all came out later, at your trial, of course. People couldn't wait to spill the beans then, could they? Racking their brains to think of all the crazy things you'd ever done. To say they'd always known what an evil, nasty piece of work you were. The prosecution even dragged up the stupid paintball gun business. As evidence of murderous thoughts, I guess.

But, for the time being, we all kept our mouths shut. It shook everyone up a bit though and we all stayed away from the bridge for ages after that. Crossing it but not hanging around and certainly not playing our little games.

The campaign to 'get something done about the bridge' picked up a bit of speed after the accident, then died down, then picked up again when Connor and his moronic mates did 'moonies' and peed on passing traffic, on their way back from the pub.

After that, nothing but having the whole thing rebuilt in solid brick would do. But these things take time. And before they'd managed to do anything about it, you'd had another of your mad ideas.

'Right? Have you all got that?'

Heads start nodding at Mr Phinn and I let mine join in. Some people are packing up, wandering out. But some of us are staying for the 3 o'clock lecture with Miss Layton. She's quite young and I think this might be her first year 'cos she's dead nervous and useless and boring.

The lads usually manage to entertain themselves for a bit staring at her boobs flopping about in those ridiculous strappy T-shirts she wears. I mean if she dresses like that in winter, what's she going to be like come summer? But it doesn't look as though Graham's going to be interested in Miss Layton today. He's too busy whispering to Soppy Sarah. I mean, what does he see in her? She's a wimp. Not even very pretty, really. Apart from the hair. The hair's nice. And the green eyes, I suppose. Slimmer than me. A bit taller. Cleverer, I suppose, too. But then, most people are.

Oh, no! Oh, no! It's bones again. Miss Layton's got a couple of lads bringing her skeletons in. As if I haven't got enough skeletons lurking around!

Typical this is. Just when I needed something

interesting to keep my attention from bouncing back and forwards, from the past to the lovebirds three rows in front, what do I get? Biology! Boring, bloody bones.

Nothing to distract me. Nothing to drag my thoughts back from that bridge and the new game you invented.

It was one night on the way home from school. Almost certainly in early March after that business with Barry's wife had got you all psyched up

People had started to muck about a bit again on the bridge. Not dropping stuff. We'd been well put off that. But pulling ourselves up on the rail, hanging over. Daring each other to lean further and further. Were we mad, or what?

You always leaned further than anyone else but even you'd reached your limits and the game was starting to get a bit boring.

'Hold my bag,' you told Tracey that night, as we approached the bridge.

Tracey ever obedient, where you were concerned, held the bag.

'Crouch down,' you told Liam.

Liam crouched down.

'Not like that!' you said, pushing him into position.

Head tucked under. Back slightly arched.

You used his back as a step and, of course, he didn't move. Didn't complain. Nobody ever complained, did they? Nobody ever tried to stop you. Not really. But then, you probably wouldn't have listened if they had.

Anyway, with his head tucked in, tortoise style, Liam was the only one who couldn't see what you were doing.

The only one who didn't see you grip the bar, swing your right leg over until you were sitting astride the flaming thing with the traffic roaring past below.

'Oh, my God, oh, my God,' breathed Tracey.

Your legs were gripping the sides, your hands tight on the bar in front of you. The bar was pretty wide. Fairly chunky. Much thicker than the bars everyone walked across in PE lessons. But then, in PE lessons, the bar was only 40cm or so off the ground. And with no articulated lorries racing along underneath.

'Alex, get down,' someone said, sort of half-heartedly.

But you didn't like being told what to do, so you only grinned.

'Bet you I can make it all the way across,' you said.

There were no takers. Because no one wanted to encourage that sort of lunacy? Or because they thought they'd lose the bet? Because you'd already started to move. Easing yourself along, painfully, agonizingly slowly.

'What the hell!' a deep voice suddenly shouted and this bloke comes racing up to us.

Not someone we knew, so you just grinned at him. Cool or what?

The guy grabbed hold of you. Lifted you down.

'You little idiot,' he said. 'You stupid, stupid little idiot.'

His face had gone all sort of purple and he was shaking. Chances are, he'd have marched you straight off to the cop shop if you hadn't kicked him in the groin. Which was the cue for everyone else to come out of their little trance and make a bolt for it.

The bloke didn't know who we were but he'd recognized our sweatshirts, so the cops were back in school the next day.

They'd got a fair description of you but no proof. Especially as the bloke couldn't even make out whether you were a boy or a girl.

'Bloody cheek!' you muttered.

But you were pleased really 'cos it meant you got away with a lecture shared with other blond, blue-eyed types of both sexes who fitted the bill.

The cops took it pretty seriously, for a while. Every time we crossed the bridge on our way to and from school, there was a cop car parked underneath and sometimes a cop actually standing on the bridge, like a 'bloody troll', you said.

The Dragon did her bit too. I can't count the number of talks we had about road safety or the number of boring videos we had to sit through.

There were letters to the paper, letters to MPs and promises that the bridge would be made safe.

And now we're back down the 'if only' route again, aren't we? If only they'd actually started the work in April, like they'd promised. But there was some problem over money or something. If only the cops had hung around, doing their patrols for longer. But they were understaffed and I guess they had other things to deal with. If only Connor hadn't nicked your idea...

'Connor crossed the bridge on the bar last night,' Liam Bradbury informed us at school one morning.

'Nice try, Liam,' you said, silencing everyone's gasps. 'But you don't catch me out that easy! I'm no April Fool.'

'S'not an April Fool,' whined Liam. 'Honest. He did it. On the way back from the pub. My sister was there. Said her heart were in her mouth 'cos he were dead pissed.'

'You'd have to be,' said Tracey. 'To try summat like that.'

'Rubbish,' you said. 'I nearly did it!'

'No, you didn't,' said Liam. 'You didn't even get halfway. Not even quarter way!'

'I would have if that bloke—'

'No you wouldn't,' said Tracey. 'You'd have bottled out.'

'Rubbish,' you said again. 'I mean it'd be easy, wouldn't it? Anyone could do it. That bar's so wide, you could walk across it!'

'Oh yeah!' said Liam. 'I'd like to see you try it.'

'OK,' you said, calm as anything. 'When?'

And it makes me feel sick to even think about it. The idea of you trying to make the walk across the top of that bridge.

But you were dead confident. You'd spent most of your life playing in dangerous places, on building sites, crawling across garage roofs, splashing about in the canal. I don't think the word danger meant anything to you at all. Or to the rest of the jerks who egged you on.

There was no doubt in anyone's mind. You were going to do it. We'd set the date, the time, everything. No point doing something like that if you weren't going to have an audience, witnesses, was there?

And was it really your fault that it all went so wrong?

84

Was it your fault that your two ugly step-sisters were both rushed into hospital at about the same time?

Trouble had been brewing since their mum upped and left at the beginning of March, without leaving so much as a note. Barry tracked her down quickly enough. It wasn't difficult. She was hiding out with her sister up in Glasgow. She'd had a 'bit of a breakdown', the sister said and wasn't going nowhere till she'd got herself sorted out.

So the freaks had to stay with you, didn't they? And you didn't like it. Not one little bit. But then, neither did anyone else, except perhaps poor Denzil, who didn't know where he was half the time. Not even Barry wanted his creepy brood around permanently and it showed. The way he was on the phone to his wife every hour, asking if she was better. As if he cared!

All he cared about was dumping his kids and I guess they must have known that too. And it couldn't have been very nice for them, could it? Oddball, despite the tarty way she dressed was only just turned thirteen. Barely older than you. And, with her weight down to under six stone, she was falling prey to every bug going, so no one was really surprised when she ended up in hospital.

But losing her sister, her mouthpiece, set The Tomato off and her skin flared up, completely out of control. Her face was so red and swollen and flaky and blotchy, you could barely tell it was a face at all.

Did you feel sorry for them? Did you heck! If anything I reckon you were jealous of the attention they were getting. Mad that your mum insisted on going with

85

Barry to the hospital three or four times a week, usually leaving you with poor, crazy, little Denzil, bouncing off the furniture shrieking 'doop, doop, people doople' or whatever his buzz phrase of the time was.

The shrinks claimed later that it was all tied in. Your feelings about your step-family. Your desire to self-destruct. That it made you even more determined to do the walk across the top of the bridge, even though Oddball and The Tomato were still in hospital on that Saturday night, even though it meant turning up at the bridge, at eight o'clock, with Denzil scurrying along behind you.

A hyper-active three-year-old, bouncing and shrieking when you were supposed to climb up on that rail. Totally focused. Total concentration. Eyes fixed firmly in front. Never daring to look down.

'OK,' you told Liam, after you'd done your checks for cops or passers-by. 'Crouch down. Properly! Stick your head in.'

'Vrrrmmm. Vrrrrmmm. Vrrroooom.'

'Shut him up, can't you!' you yelled at Tracey, as Denzil raced round in circles making car noises.

You were up there. Sitting astride the top of the bridge. You pulled one foot up, pressing down with your hands, holding yourself steady. Ready to make the stand.

'Nee-naw, nee-naw, nee-naw.'

'I said, shut him up,' you yelled, as Denzil shrieked and clung onto the rails, trying to shake them.

He couldn't move them, of course. The bridge wasn't that badly made. But the mere thought of that bridge shaking was enough, I guess. Your foot went down.

'I can't do it,' you said. 'Not with him looping around.'

You stared down defiantly at your mates. What was it you saw on their faces, Alex? Relief? Disappointment?

'I'll go across,' you said, desperately trying to save face. 'But not the walk. Not tonight. But I'll shuffle across.'

You did too. Hands out in front of you. Dead steady. Easing yourself across.

Shuffling along, with everyone praying that none of the drivers would look up. That the cops wouldn't pick tonight to do one of their spot checks. That no pedestrians would need to cross the bridge. That Tracey would be able to hold onto Denzil for long enough to keep him fairly still and quiet. That you wouldn't fall.

You didn't. You made it all the way to the other side. Swung your leg back over. Jumped down. Punched the air with your fists. Let your mates gather round, congratulating you. But it wasn't really good enough, was it, Alex?

It had been done before. Your mates knew that. You knew that. You'd only done what Connor had done. And only being eleven to his nineteen wasn't much of a consolation, was it? And I guess everyone knew what was in your mind. That you were still determined to make the walk. And maybe you would have done if Denzil...

'Shit, that's my toe!'

'Sorry,' says the great ape who's just trodden on me in his rush to get out of the lecture hall.

'It's all right,' I say, bending forward to rub my foot. 'It's all right.'

And I mean it. The pain in my toe, the creak of seats, the rustle of bags as people tramp out has pulled me back from the edge of somewhere I really didn't wanted to be.

Even the sight of Graham and Sarah staggering to their feet, arms clumsily draped round each other, is a relief. The petty problems of the present are nothing compared to where I've just been. Where I was about to go. What I was about to see.

If I'm quick, I can get out before Graham and Sarah pick up their bags. Tomorrow I'll be fine again. I'll even smile at them and ask them for their lecture notes. Pretend I fell asleep or something 'cos I haven't a clue what's been going on for the past hour.

For now, I just want to get out. Go home.

It's stopped raining. People are standing in groups in the quadrangle, chatting. The noise sort of freaks me a bit and, for a minute, I'm all disorientated. Don't know whether I'm supposed to be turning left or right. The buildings in this part of the college are all fairly new. They all look the same, so it's easy to get confused sometimes, especially when your mind's been somewhere else entirely for the past hour.

'Alex! Hang on. Wait for us!'

I swing round, Soppy Sarah's shriek echoing in my ears.

I'm staring straight into her face. Into Graham's face. But they're not looking at me. They're looking past me. To the guy coming out of the library.

Alexander Fraser.

They were shouting to him, not me. Alex is a boy's

name too. Alexander, they wanted. Not Alexina.

How could they have been shouting to me? They don't know me, do they? They don't know about Alexina. They only know Josie.

But their eyes are focused on me now. And I can feel my mouth opening and closing, as the blood drains from my face.

'I'm Josie!' I say. 'I'm Josie!'

'Er, I know,' says Graham.

He looks embarrassed. Like this is about him. Him and Sarah. Him and Josie. Me.

'You didn't want me,' I say, shaking my head. 'You wanted Alex. I'm not Alex. I'm Josie. I'm Josie.'

Chapter 9

I don't know how I've got home. Same way as usual, I guess, but I don't remember the bus or the train. I just remember rushing out of that quadrangle.

Why's the door locked? Why doesn't Moira answer the bell? She's chosen today to put her decorations up and the flashing lights round the door are doing my head in. Come on, Moira. Open the door.

Then I remember. Dentist. She's gone with Lara to the dentist, 'cos Lara doesn't like dentists and there's no chance she'll go on her own.

'I'll leave the key under the loose stone,' Moira had told me that morning.

The loose stone on the side wall. And sure enough the key is there. But I can hardly hold it, let alone turn it in the lock, 'cos my hands are still shaking.

Did Graham and Sarah realize? Did they know I'd answered to that name? Or would they think it was co-incidence that I'd turned round? Possibly, if I hadn't kept repeating those words.

'I'm Josie. I'm Josie.'

I don't know how many times I said it before I finally came to my senses and tore myself away. Why did I say that? Why did I keep saying it? Who was I trying to

90

convince? Them? Myself?

The door's open and there's a massive Christmas tree in the hall that wasn't there this morning. Lights off but glittering with baubles and tinsel. Moira's been busy. But I can't stop to look, even if I wanted to, 'cos I know I'm going to be sick.

I'm not sick. I keep retching but nothing comes except the bitter bile lurking down the back of my throat. I think about cleaning my teeth, but it seems too difficult, too much trouble.

One term. I didn't even last my first term without making a mistake. What if they talk? What if they put two and two together? What if they remember the original story? What if they make the connection? What if they recognize me?

'Look in the mirror, Josie. Look in the mirror.'

I listen to the voice. My voice? Alex's voice? Josie's voice? I force myself to stare in the bathroom mirror.

Greyish eyes stare back at me and you'd have to look real close to spot the coloured lenses which mask the real baby blue. Hair long and dark. Not blonde and nothing like the bizarre cuts Alex used to have – the closely shaved scalp, the spiky crop. Or grown slightly longer, slightly more feminine, for the trial. When they even made you wear cute little hair slides, for heaven's sake!

My face has thinned out too. One of the natural changes which came with age and less junk food in my diet. Still sort of pretty, I guess, but I've lost the little blonde cherub look.

So there's not much left of Alex. Not on the outside. Nothing that anyone could recognize. Is there?

There's not supposed to be much left on the inside, either. That's what seven years of counselling, therapy, education, incarceration, probing and analysis were about, weren't they? Taking you apart. Putting you back together again. A different you. A better you. Only it's not that simple, is it?

Wash in. Wash out. Wash over. Like the hair dye. Is that all it is? Is that all they did? Am I still you, inside, Alex? Is that why I can't let go?

I take off my shoe, hammer on the mirror, trying to break it. But it doesn't even crack. Wrong kind of shoe. Wrong kind of mirror. Who knows?

My room. There must be something in my room. Nothing on the dressing table, on the surfaces, so I start pulling out drawers, tipping their contents onto the floor. After my last episode with the pins, Moira went through my room with me. Chucking out anything sharp, anything dangerous. Even pouring some of my perfume from glass to plastic bottles, so it smells all sort of funny and tainted now. But there must be something. There has to be.

No use trying the kitchen. Moira keeps the knife drawer locked. Even little things like corkscrews are locked away. She knows how inventive I can be when I'm desperate.

Then I remember. Something I saw when I came in.

Most of the Christmas tree decorations are plastic but the lights and some of the baubles are glass. Maybe not proper glass. I don't know. But they're sharp, easy to crush in my bare hands. I feel them cut into my palm before I sit down on the bottom stair, pick out the little bits of wire and roll up my sleeve.

'You wouldn't believe it,' Moira says, bursting in through the front door which I've left unlocked. 'Lara bit the dentist! She only went and bit him, didn't she?'

'It was an accident,' Lara protests. 'I just closed my mouth and his hand was still there.'

Moira and Lara are both laughing, so I guess his injury wasn't too bad, but they stop laughing as soon as they see what I'm doing. In fact Lara bursts into tears.

'It's all right, Lara,' Moira tells her. 'It's all right. You go and make us a nice cup of tea, eh?'

Lara stumbles towards the kitchen, still crying, and Moira sits down next to me, taking the glittering green glass fragment from my hand before I have a chance to cut deep.

'Oh, Josie,' she says.

'I'm not Josie, though, am I?' I hear myself scream. 'I'm Alex. I'll always be bloody Alex.'

That scream went on in my head for days. It wasn't only the lights and baubles that were in pieces. It was me. No chance of me going back to college for the last couple of days of term. I couldn't even get myself out of the house. I don't think I even moved off the stairs for hours.

I've got vague memories of Moira sitting there, washing the bits out of my hands. Putting TCP cream on. The damage wasn't too bad at all. Not by my standards. Moira called the doctor who increased my tablets – the ones that are supposed to keep me calm! But maybe he increased them too much 'cos I don't remember anything about the next few days. I mean nothing at all. Except the scream.

Moira says I slept most of the time. She left me to it at first but then got a bit panicky and asked the doctor if we could cut back on the pills. It seemed to do the trick and by Christmas Day I was functioning well enough to pull a cracker and not mind too much when Lara stuck a stupid paper hat on my head.

Most students go home for Christmas but not me or Lara. Where would we go? Like I said, Lara's been in care most of her life and me . . . well, I haven't heard from my mum since the day I got put away, have I?

Sometimes I kid myself that she wants to see me. That she still thinks about me. That she still cares. That it's fear of Barry that stops her making contact. What he'd do to her, if he found her. What he'd do to me.

But I know that's not true. She doesn't want to see me. And when I'm being really, really straight with myself, I know I can't blame her.

So, things being as they are, I didn't expect any Christmas presents and I was dead surprised when I saw the little pile under the tree. Chocolates from Lara, bath gels from my social worker and a whole load of stuff from Moira and Frank. Nothing big. Nothing expensive but enough to make me cry.

'Jesus doesn't want you to be sad on his birthday,' Lara informed me.

So I tried to get a grip. For her, more than Jesus, of course.

Moira kept everything pretty light over Christmas. I reckon she's had enough of her 'special' students to know that Christmas can be a bit of a dodgy time. Especially when your last seven Christmases have been spent in a Young Offenders Secure Unit.

But I can't let myself get into the 'poor me' routine. That was something they hammered into me in the unit. Don't blame circumstances. Don't blame everyone else. Take responsibility. Face up to what you did.

Well, I thought I had. *They* thought I had or they wouldn't have let me out, would they? Only I'm not so sure anymore.

Apparently I'd told Moira what had freaked me, sometime in those first few days, in between my long sleeps. I don't remember telling her but she had a fair grasp of the situation, so I guess I must have done.

Later on, after we'd got all the jolly festive bit out of the way, she went back to it, in preparation for my return to college next term. Moira's confident I'll be able to go back. She says she's a hundred per cent certain that Graham and Sarah won't have clocked anything. That they'd just think I was being freaky after seeing them together. The only thing that's stopping me going back is my own fear, Moira says.

So she delves back with me into the lecture hall.

Seeing you turn into Mr Phinn. Seeing the picture of the bridge up on the screen. Slipping back into the past. Stopping, as always, before the crucial moment.

And the point is, I stopped when I was talking to Moira too. I couldn't take it that little bit further. I couldn't actually talk about what you did. YOU. I'm doing it again, see? Detaching myself. 'Cos it's all so confusing. I'm supposed to face up to what y... to what I did. But I'm supposed to move on too. Be me not her. Josie, not Alex. Is it any wonder I'm going crazy?

'You're not crazy, Josie,' Moira tells me, as if she really believes it.

'So why do I still have to see a shrink every month?'

'A counsellor, not a shrink,' she points out. 'And it's just to help you to keep going forward. To keep on the right track.'

Right track! I've just had a major bloody derailment and I'm expected to go back to college like nothing's happened.

There'd been a case meeting the day after New Year's Day to which I wasn't invited. One of my regular 'reviews' which was brought forward 'cos of what happened. And they're all quite confident that I haven't broken any of the rules attached to my release. That I'm not posing a danger to anybody, except perhaps myself.

Trouble is, I think I'm going backwards, not forwards. Back to the time, just after my arrest, when I couldn't face up to anything at all.

'I didn't do it,' I kept repeating. 'I didn't do it. It wasn't me.'

Not an exactly convincing defence when there were a dozen witnesses, at least. But, the thing was, I believed it. Really believed it.

'Self-delusion,' the psychologist called it.

So, when I finally started to get a grip, to say what I really meant, they thought that was self-delusion too.

'I didn't *mean* it. I didn't mean to do it. I didn't mean it. It was an accident.'

Was it though? Was it, Alex?

The jury didn't think so.

Three years later, in the unit, we decided the jury was right. And that was the 'turning point'. That was what the staff wanted to hear. They were so pleased with me, I couldn't backtrack after that. Not even when they made me go through it all again, over and over in 'therapy', analysing every second, like I was doing it all over again.

How I felt when I failed to make that walk across the bridge, with my mates all staring at me, their little mouths hanging open in disappointment. Disappointment that I'd only shuffled across! Done what none of them could have done in a million years! And they're looking at me, like it was nothing.

'So, how did you feel?'

'Angry.'

Took me years to be able to say that word.

'And who were you angry with?'

'Denzil.'

The word was out of my mouth before I could stop it.

97

I was angry with Denzil because his prattling had made me lose my nerve. Or had it? Or did I know, as soon as I put my foot up on that rail, as soon as I tried to stand, that I wasn't going to do it? Way before Denzil started his 'vrmmm, vrmmm'.

Did I know when I started to climb up again, after my shuffle, that it was only bravado? Was I secretly pleased when Denzil started up again? Dead right I was.

'I want to do it! I want to do it, Alex! Me try!' Denzil screamed.

'Right!' I said, leaping down. 'You try then, seeing as you won't let me! Let's see how brave you are, eh?'

I lifted him up, sat him astride the rail. That's all I meant to do. Just let him sit there for a second or two. Holding onto him.

'You must have known it was dangerous!'

The dozens of voices that have said that over the years scream out at me and I cover my ears with my hands.

But I'm almost there now. I'm not going to stop.

'I didn't know,' I hear myself scream back at them. 'I didn't think! I was holding onto him! I was holding on!'

Somehow, though, the rail was higher than I thought and Denzil heavier. It was a struggle to get him up there and I remember the sudden thud in my chest as I thought I was losing my grip. But I wouldn't have done. I stretched up, clutched him tighter. I wouldn't have lost my hold. I wouldn't. Not if he'd sat still.

'Vrrmm, vrmmm,' he starts yelling, like he was astride

a motorbike or something. 'Vrmmm. Vrrmmm.'

'Get him down, Alex,' someone breathed as Denzil started to sway.

Deliberately swaying! Like he hadn't a clue where he really was. How high up he was.

'Get him down, Alex!'

Why me? Why didn't they help? Why didn't they do something? Maybe because they'd already heard the siren in the distance.

'Nee-naw, nee-naw,' Denzil shrieks, kicking out as I try to pull him back by his leg.

'Keep still, you stupid—'

I swore. Sure I swore. Dozens of words spilling out after each other. But not in anger. I swear it wasn't anger I was spitting out. It was fear. Feeling the cloth of his jeans slip through my hands. Knowing it wasn't flesh I was holding anymore.

They said I pushed him! Panicked when the police car came into view. Pushed him off the bridge, down onto the busy road and tried to run.

Did you, Alex? Was it like they said? Was all the anger you'd been bottling up over the years suddenly directed against Denzil in one final shove? Was it worse than that? As bad as the prosecution made out? Was it pre-meditated? Was it in your mind all along? To take Denzil to that bridge. Could you have planned it, like you once planned the worm sandwiches, the brick and the paintball attack, as some sort of crazy revenge?

You could. You know you could. You were capable of

planning it. Capable of later blotting it out. Just like they said you did.

Or should I believe you? The whimpering, pathetic voice that still cries out to me.

'It was an accident, Josie. I didn't mean to. I didn't. Not Denzil. He was just a kid. A baby! I wouldn't have done that. Not on purpose. It was an accident.'

'You can't hide, Alex!' I hear myself say. 'Don't try to hide behind me! I won't protect you. I know what you did. And I hate you, Alex. Can you hear me? I hate you.'

I'm still hearing myself scream as my hands go up to my face, nails pulling downwards, tearing my flesh.

Chapter 10

Moira doesn't find me soon enough this time. My face is a mess. Reason enough not to go back to college tomorrow.

At first she thinks it's all to do with that, of not wanting to face Graham and Sarah. Till I tell her where I've been.

Not just on the bridge, feeling Denzil slip away from me. But further. Much further.

Hearing the horns, the screams, the brakes, the gut churning thud of metal on metal, the sirens. Trying to run. Not getting very far 'cos the cops are already there. Were on their way even before I lifted Denzil onto the rail. Alerted by a passing motorist who'd seen kids 'mucking about on that bridge again'.

Feeling a sort of out-of-body experience, as they led me away, as though none of it had anything to do with me. Not the ambulances, or the fire engines, or the dozens of police vehicles, or Denzil's crushed and mangled body, or the other carnage under that bridge.

Not knowing, not wanting to know, how bad it was. Not really taking it in for days, weeks, months, years even.

That's what got the European Court of Human Rights on my side, eventually. They said I didn't know what was going on at my trial. And they were right.

They've changed the rules now for trials involving kids. Tried to make it more child friendly. Children can talk through a video link instead of going to the courtroom. Judges don't wear their wigs.

But it wasn't the wigs and freaky clothes that got to me. It was what they were saying. What they were trying to get me to say. Get me to see.

Numbers were meaningless. Nine cars and a lorry involved in the pile up. Nine people taken to hospital with minor injuries. A further four with serious injuries. One who later died in hospital, adding to the three who'd died at the scene. Bringing the total fatalities to four.

Fatalities. I think the police actually used that word when they were questioning me and then, later, at the trial but I wouldn't have understood. Not even when it was spelt out to me.

Four people died because of what I did.

Terrible enough. I was the girl accused of pushing her three-year-old step-brother to his death from a bridge. Of causing the deaths of three others.

But the truly terrible thing, the prosecution said, was that I showed no remorse. No concern for any of the victims. Only myself.

How could I tell them? How could I explain? I didn't have the words then. I'm not sure I have them now. Words to describe the shut down, the paralysis that gripped me, freezing all thoughts, all emotions. I didn't understand. I didn't want to understand. It wasn't me. I couldn't have done that. Not to Denzil. Not to those other people. I couldn't have.

Even when the jury delivered its verdict. Guilty on one charge of murder, three charges of manslaughter, it was like they were talking about someone else, somewhere else.

'I'm not trying to make excuses,' I tell Moira, in my garbled attempt to explain.

She nods. She knows I understand now, understand the horror of what I did. The lives I destroyed. She knows that's why I scratch and cut myself.

The cutting and gouging started in the unit. It got worse and worse once the messages had started to sink in, once I began to think about the people who'd died. The old couple who were setting off on their first holiday since their retirement, who never even made it to the airport. The off-duty cop, who died in hospital, whose colleagues got the message about him while they were still questioning me in that holding cell. And Denzil, of course.

Denzil was the reason I got named in court. I started the trial as 'child X', protected because I was a minor. A child who 'couldn't be named for legal reasons'. But Barry wasn't having any of that, was he? He burst out of the court and waved my photograph in front of the TV cameras that were waiting. Shouted my name. Swore he was going to kill me.

He was arrested but never charged. And as soon as they released him, he was at it again. Spreading the word in any way he could, whipping up public anger, hysteria. So it was pointless not to name me.

Barry broke all the rules but he got away with it 'cos I guess public sympathy was with him. Him and his wife, Oddball and The Tomato, back together, as a family. United in grief. Spilling out their stories to the newspapers after I was sentenced. So my mum became the tart who'd enticed him away. Me, the mad, dangerous demon who'd murdered their son. Barry, the grief-stricken bloody hero. He even blamed Oddball's eating disorder and The Tomato's speech and skin problems on what happened to Denzil. Bloody liar!

But a lot of people believed him. And I think the worst thing about the trial wasn't the questions or the court-room, it was being taken there each day in the back of that van, handcuffed to a cop, hearing the stones, the missiles, crash against the side of the van. Hearing the shouts.

'Murderer, murderer.'

Maybe they were right. Maybe I deserved it after what I did. But I was eleven years old. Eleven. Sitting in the back of that van screaming and crying.

No one ever saw that. But they saw Oddball and The Tomato dressed solemnly in black. They saw Barry with his tears. Those are the tears the public remember. And there's still a lot of sympathy for him out there. So he got a fair bit of support for his recent campaign to keep me locked away. To get me moved to an adult prison when I was eighteen. And there was a big public outcry when they let me out.

In some ways I reckon the public are harder on child criminals than they are on adults. They've got these cosy views about childhood innocence, I guess. So it scares them, it really scares them, when a kid does something bad. It's an affront to nature. They want to hide it away. Lock it up.

Funny how they don't seem to realize that Barry's more psychotic than I ever was. That he means those threats. Against me. Against my mum, wherever she is.

Whoever she is, now.

Mum would probably have had to change her name, anyway. Move away. Try to start over. Barry beating her up, the day after my arrest, just sort of clinched the matter.

He got away with that too. 'Cos Mum wouldn't even say who'd done it, would she? Probably 'cos she was scared he'd do worse if she told. Or maybe part of her still loved him. But I can't think about that 'cos it makes me sick. Physically sick.

But not as sick as when I wonder whether part of her still loves me.

Or should I say you? Because she doesn't know me, does she? She doesn't know Josie at all. Doesn't want to. She's made that plain enough.

I wrote her letters while I was in the unit. Letters which the staff said they'd forward to her. Letters that came back, unopened.

Moira hands me a tissue for the tears I don't even realize are there till they start to drip into my scratches, making them sting.

She tells me this is normal. Normal! That there'll be

105

times when I need to go through it all over again.

'And each time, you'll be able to move on that little bit further,' she tells me.

Maybe Moira's right. Maybe going to hell and back has helped. Or maybe it's Moira who's helped... again. I don't know what they pay her for looking after me and Lara but whatever it is, it's not enough.

She's had a really rotten cold and I know she was totally knackered after Christmas but it didn't stop her. She still spent hours talking it all through with me. In the early days of the New Year, when I couldn't go back to college, she made me focus on me, on Josie.

For the first few days, I couldn't. Couldn't push myself forward. I was stuck, somewhere in the recent past, in the unit, when I was neither Josie nor Alex.

I was Gemma in there. Not a name I liked. It's a nice enough name but it just never felt like me and I couldn't quite see why I couldn't carry on being Alex, until they told me I needed protection. From the other girls as much as anything. Not that any of them were exactly saints. They'd robbed, mugged, mutilated, even murdered. But even they drew the line somewhere. And that somewhere was murdering little children.

So it was Gemma who went to classes where there were only four other kids and two teachers. Quiet, scared little Gemma who sat on her own and got on with whatever they wanted her to do. Made progress too. Got to be quite clever, Gemma did. Hiding behind a name.

106

Only letting Alex creep out at night, whispering to her in the dark. Or suddenly losing control, letting Alex burst out all wild and crazy during therapy. Gemma and Alex fighting for control.

Moira finds it strange the way I do this. Talk about Alex, Gemma, Josie as though they're three different people. She tries not to let it show but I know she finds it a bit creepy.

But that's the way it is to me. And maybe that makes me more than a touch crazy but the shrink insists I'm not schizophrenic. That I don't have multiple personalities. No psychological disorder that you could actually put a name to.

'We all have different sides to our character,' she tells me. 'It's just that you give yours names.'

Well, that's all right then, isn't it?

But she should try living in the battle zone that's my head sometimes. Trying to stop Gemma cutting and slashing, trying to stop Alex from surfacing at all. Trying to be Josie. Whoever she is.

Josie's OK, according to Moira. Josie's the person who started to emerge in the unit before she even had her new name. She's not perfect. She still gets angry sometimes but she can manage her anger. She still gets frightened but she can handle that too, with a bit of help. She's no genius but she's smart enough to do well.

And before I know how she's done it, Moira's got me thinking about the future again. About me. About my ambition.

I want to be a zookeeper when I finish college. I've never even been to a zoo. Can you believe that? We didn't have many cosy family outings when I was a kid. And later in the unit when I was allowed the odd day out, it was mainly functional stuff like shopping. Simple things to get me used to being on the outside again.

If I stick with college, I'll get to do trips like that next year. Even a bit of work experience, which will be great 'cos I can really see myself as a zookeeper. I like being out and about and a bit of muck doesn't bother me. Couldn't imagine Soppy Sarah splashing about in wellies, knee deep in elephant dung somehow, but I wouldn't mind. That's the Alex part of me, I suppose. The tom-boy who used to roll about on a muddy football field, shrieking and laughing. One of the few bits of Alex I'm happy to live with.

And I wouldn't mind what sort of animals they gave me to work with. I got to be pretty good with everything at the Animal Therapy Centre, not just the cuddlies. I was the only one who'd clean out the stick insects or catch the frogs when they escaped.

But it's primates that really fascinate me. Not that we had any chimps or gorillas at the animal centre but I've read a lot and seen loads of videos about them. It was a David Attenborough documentary on mountain gorillas that got me interested. That one where he gets up real close to a silver-back male. I can watch that one over and over.

They look so human, don't they? Those gorillas. And sure, it's best if animals like that are in the wild. But the trouble is, they're not, are they? Because they're being poached. All their habitats are being destroyed, and it makes me really mad.

But Moira says that's OK, to focus your anger on issues, rather than on more personal stuff.

Alex wouldn't have cared about pollution or destruction of the environment, wouldn't have even known about it. Gemma went through a phase of believing zoos were wrong, that it was cruel to keep animals locked up. But then one of the tutors got her interested in the conservation and breeding programmes that were going on in zoos and that was it. She was hooked. I was hooked.

My college tutors warn me that there aren't many jobs in zoos around. That there are hundreds of applicants for each one. But I'm determined to do it, as I tell Moira.

'I'd do anything,' I say. 'Anything to be able to work in a zoo.'

Anything, as Moira patiently points out, includes getting back to college. Getting those exams. And she's promised me that when the weather picks up, we'll have a trip to the zoo. Her and me and Lara 'cos Lara likes animals too.

So I've got to get back to college, haven't I? I've missed two weeks of this term already but the scratches on my face have almost healed and when I slap a bit of make-up on they're barely noticeable at all. So I've got no excuse now.

Scary thought, though, going back. Not so much the work, 'cos I've been keeping up at home. But just facing people again.

Thanks to Moira's phone call, they all think I've had the 'flu bug that's been going round. So maybe it won't be too difficult. And, as for Graham and Sarah . . . well, Moira's almost persuaded me that they couldn't possibly have registered anything. That they won't have given my ravings, two days before the end of term, a second thought.

'Josie?'

The whisper is so faint, I think it's a voice in my mind again, until I see Lara's head appear round the door.

'I've got some bread,' she says, appearing with a plastic bag. 'Do you want to come and feed the ducks with me?'

I start to shake my head. She's always asking me but I never go. I don't like the park. Or, if I'm being honest with myself, I don't like the bridge you have to cross to get there. I'll still go miles and miles out of my way to avoid a bridge.

'Please,' Lara says. 'It's getting dark. Moira says I shouldn't go on my own. And if I don't go the ducks will be hungry.'

'OK,' I say, though I know there's not a chance of those ducks going hungry. Dozens of people must feed them.

Such a big response to such a little word! Lara's face positively blazes with gratitude as she rushes to get my coat.

So it's worth it. Lara's happy. The ducks will be happy, I guess. And if I bottle out at the bridge, what the heck. We can always walk the long way round.

We do walk the long way round and it's as unnerving

as it always is, being out with Lara, because people stare. I used to freak 'cos I thought it was me they were staring at, as if they recognized me, as if they knew. Then I started to realize, it wasn't that sort of long, lingering, 'do I know that person' sort of stare.

It was a brief, quick, 'oh dear we shouldn't be looking', turn your eyes away stare. An 'isn't it a shame' sort of stare. And I always want to thump them.

I don't, of course, because my anger management kicks in. I link arms with Lara as we walk down the road, swinging our bag of bread.

'Why do you hurt yourself?' she says, suddenly spoiling the illusion that everything's OK.

This is the first time Lara's ever said anything about my cutting and scratching. She notices, she gets upset, but she's never spoken about it before. And I don't know what to say. I don't want to snap at her, don't want to lie to her, don't want to upset her. Which doesn't leave too many options.

'You shouldn't hurt yourself,' she says, tired of waiting for an answer.

'No,' I agree.

'You won't do it again, will you?' she asks.

'I hope not,' is the best I can manage.

Chapter 11

Funny how time plays tricks. This term seems to have gone much quicker than the last. Possibly because I started it late and Easter's quite early this year. Possibly just because I'm really, really enjoying it. Days only seem to last about five hours, whereas in the unit they lasted at least fifty!

But I'm not thinking about any of that. I'm really moving forward now.

Everyone was dead nice when I got back, falling over themselves to make sure I caught up on any bits and pieces I'd missed.

Some people were a bit too nice. Soppy Sarah for one. Her and Graham are still together and I guess she maybe feels a bit guilty. Or maybe she doesn't even know he ever asked me out. Maybe she's just trying to branch out, make a few more friends.

Because I tend to forget that the first term was probably as hard for normal people as it was for me. We were all strangers. All new. All nervous. So even raving extroverts like Sarah might have been a bit wobbly and unsure underneath.

She's pretty sure of herself now though. She's become quite the centre of attention, has Sarah. Organizing everyone to go bowling, see a film, go for a pizza. Whatever. And she's not the sort of person it's easy to say no to, so I've sort of found myself tagging along.

That's all it was at first. Tagging along. Hovering on the fringes. Hoping no one would speak to me.

Recently though I've started to 'come out of myself a bit', as Sarah so patronizingly puts it. I'm even better when Sarah's not around, when I'm just with Alison and Dina, 'cos they're a bit of a laugh, those two. Graham's OK, of course. And Mark. But I'm not so keen on Liam 'cos he's a bit loud and over the top and every time someone says his name it makes me think of Liam Bradbury. But I guess I can't go through the rest of my life avoiding people called Liam or Tracey or Barry or Gemma just 'cos they remind me of things I'd rather forget.

Sometimes Alexander Fraser hangs round with us but luckily he's really into sport which takes up a lot of his time. 'Cos it's agony when he's around. Hearing that name.

Alex. Alex. Alex.

Trying not to respond, even with a twitch of a muscle or flicker of an eye.

Moira says it's 'nice' that I've started to make some friends. That it's good I'm getting out a bit more. The only time she wasn't so thrilled was last week, when it was Alison's birthday. I got a bit carried away with the celebrations and puked up on the new white rug Moira's just bought for the lounge.

It wasn't so much the stains she was worried about or the dry cleaning bill. It was me. So I got a bit of a long lecture on the evils of drink. As if I didn't know! But fears for my liver didn't worry me as much as fears about my tongue. And I got all sort of panicky for a bit wondering what I might have said, while I was staggering round that club. What I might have said about you.

Stop it, Josie, stop it!

Concentrate on the conversation. What's the point of hanging round with a bunch of mates if you're not going to listen to a word they say? If you're going to keep wandering off down nightmare lane?

'Oh, my God, they've done it!' Alison's saying.

'What?' said Mark, who obviously hasn't been paying attention either.

'Killed him,' says Alison, nodding towards the TV screen which constantly mutters to itself in the corner of the college coffee bar. 'That bloke in America who shot all those kiddies. They've killed him by lethal injection. He didn't get his reprieve.'

'Good,' says Sarah. 'People like that just don't deserve to live.'

I look up and try to listen to what they're saying on the news but I can't because Alison's opened up a whole debate of our own.

'Yeah,' says Dina. 'We ought to bring back the death penalty here for people like that.'

'So we can be as bad as the murderers, right?' says Mark. 'An eye for an eye and all that rot.'

'No! As a deterrent. To make people think twice before they go on a shooting spree.'

'But it doesn't, does it? People who do stuff like that are usually sick, aren't they? They don't exactly think rationally, do they?'

'Yeah and what about people who are convicted and later found to be innocent? Doesn't help them much if they've already been hanged or electrocuted, does it?'

'Yeah, well, there aren't many cases like that. And what about the victims? Don't they deserve some justice? I get dead sick of people bleating about the rights of criminals all the time. They don't deserve any rights!'

Comments bouncing back and forward till I'm dizzy trying to make out who's saying what.

'What do you reckon, Alex?'

I open my mouth. Snap it shut again as Alex Fraser answers.

'Dunno, really,' he says. 'I mean it's sort of complicated, in'it?'

So he's not really added much to the debate but it doesn't matter because everyone else has got plenty to say. And every comment's making the throb in my head louder and the pain across my chest tighter. I want to get out of there but I don't think I can physically move.

'If a dog turns nasty,' Sarah was saying, 'you have it put down, don't you? If it's savaged one kid, you don't let it out on the street to go and savage another, do you?'

'We're not talking about dogs, Sarah,' Alison points out. 'And we're not talking about letting murderers out on the streets.'

The word 'murderer' seems to hover in the air and I can imagine it settling over my head.

'Aren't we?' said Sarah. 'So just how long do most of these nutters stay in prison? There was that case recently—'

And I'm almost sick in the pause that follows. I put my hand up to my mouth, terrified I'll scream if she mentions you.

'You know the one,' Sarah says, looking round. 'That bloke who battered his landlady to death. He was supposed to be serving a life sentence for a previous murder but they let him out, didn't they? He was supposed to be safe!'

'Er, it's nearly two o'clock' says Dina, looking at her watch. 'I think we ought to—'

But nobody's listening. They're listening to Graham now.

'I think Sarah's right. I'm not in favour of the death penalty but I think all murders should carry a life sentence. And it should mean just that. Life. They shouldn't ever be let out. Once they've killed there's always the chance that they'll kill again.'

And he's like looking straight at me as he speaks. Not because he knows anything but because I'm the only one who hasn't said anything so far. He's trying to draw me in.

'So you don't think people can change?' says Mark, coming to my rescue.

'Not that much, no,' says Graham. 'It's like once a tree's started to grow twisted, you can't ever straighten it out.'

Twisted. That's how I feel. Twisted, knotted up inside.

116

Maybe he's right. Maybe you can never straighten out.

'And why does it grow twisted in the first place?' says Mark. "Cos it's been dumped in lousy conditions, that's why. Like most of the people we're talking about. But change the conditions, give them education, counselling, whatever it takes, and yeah, I reckon some of 'em will change.'

'You're on the wrong course, Mark,' says Sarah, suddenly laughing, lightening up for a minute. 'You should be doing Social Work. But like all these social worker types, it's all talk really, isn't it? You might be all in favour of letting these nutters out but you'd soon complain if you ended up with one of 'em living next door to you.'

'Talking of complaints,' says Dina, flashing her watch around. 'It's gone two. I don't know about you lot but I've got a lecture to go to.'

They all start to move until there's only me and Mark left.

'You OK, Josie?' he asks.

My throat's still constricted and all I can do is nod.

'You coming then?' he says, grabbing my hand and pulling me to my feet.

He smiles at me as I stagger up. He looks down. Holds onto to my hand for a fraction longer than he needs to.

Because he doesn't know, does he? He doesn't know whose hand he's holding.

Someone's watching me. I'm sure someone's following me around.

117

It started three days ago, when I was on my way home on Wednesday night, after that debate in the coffee bar. So, at first, I though it was you, Alex. I thought I was just freaking again and I kept turning round expecting to see this blonde kid grinning and waving at me.

But you weren't there. As far as I could see there wasn't anybody there. Well, there was, of course. Hundreds of them. People in bus queues. People darting in and out of shops. People on the train. None of them seemed interested in me, even when I stopped and stood still for a while, staring.

Nothing. But the minute I moved on, I sensed it again. Felt the eyes burning into my back, heard the soft, purposeful footsteps shuffling closer.

I haven't told Moira. Haven't told anybody. Because it can't be real, can it? This is paranoia, isn't it?

This could have been my contribution to the coffee bar debate, couldn't it? What it feels like to get that reprieve. That second chance. To be allowed out.

Terrifying. Bloody terrifying. Constantly looking over your shoulder. Seeing yourself. Seeing your victims. The hazy shadows. The ghosts. Not to mention the real people. The face in the crowd who you think you recognize. Who might recognize you.

If I'd been able to think straight, if I'd been smart, I wouldn't have had to mention you or me, Alex. I could have done it without making it personal. I could have told them about Mary-Anne. Pretended it was something I'd seen on a documentary, rather than witnessed with my own eyes.

Mary-Anne stabbed her grandad to death when she was only nine years old. In the secure unit where she ended up, Mary-Anne kept a scrapbook of all the newspaper cuttings, the ones describing the monster who'd inflicted twenty-three stab wounds on a defenceless pensioner.

Only it wasn't like that, Mary-Anne said. He wasn't a defenceless pensioner, he was a dirty old man who'd heaped years of abusive misery on her mother, her sister and herself.

The trouble was, the mother and sister wouldn't back up her story. And the jury wouldn't believe she'd killed in self-defence. Twenty-three stab wounds sounded more like a wild frenzy than an attempt to protect herself.

Other girls in the unit were never quite sure. Mary-Anne could be very aggressive, scary, intimidating when the staff weren't looking. No one got too close to Mary-Anne.

She must have given a bit of a different impression to the shrinks and the parole board though, because when she was seventeen they let her out. And her whoops and shrieks must have been heard for miles around, the day she found out. She was going to have a real wild time, she told everyone. Nothing criminal. Nothing that would get her put away again. But boy was she going to make up for lost time. The booze, the parties, the shopping. She couldn't wait.

Less than a year later she was back. She wasn't sent back, though. In fact her only crime was to be caught trying to break into the unit! Breaking *in*to a prison! Can you believe that? Silly cow actually wanted to come back. She couldn't hack it on the outside. Couldn't cope.

They wouldn't let her stay, of course. And my story sort of falls down there 'cos I can't finish it. I haven't a clue what happened to Mary-Anne in the end. Did she commit a real crime to make sure she got put back inside? Did she turn to drugs, booze? Did she top herself? It's possible. Or is she out in the world somewhere, wandering around, lost, like me? Looking over her shoulder.

I'm so busy thinking about Mary-Anne that I almost miss my station and dive for the door just as someone's about to slam it shut. But I'm not the only dozy passenger. Someone crashes out, immediately behind me, almost sending me sprawling onto the platform.

I swing round ready to snarl and, in that instant, I know I haven't been imagining it. Someone has been following me. Someone's tracked me down.

Chapter 12

Barry's face looms towards me. I see his tattooed hand reach into his pocket. Try to run as I see the glint of the knife. Scream out to the passers-by but they're all hurrying to their trains or from their trains and they don't see.

They don't care as the knife slides in, so sharp, so smooth that I barely feel it at all. Would hardly know that anything's happened except that my mind's somehow detached itself from my body.

I'm looking down, but not on the railway station. On a man bleeding on a pub doorstep as a hazy figure runs away. My dad? Is it my dad? Did he do that? Was he a murderer too, like they said? Was it all there in my genes? Predestined. Is it there still?

There's a little kid running after him but the kid isn't you, Alex. It's Denzil. A thin, skeletal Denzil, with his face covered in sores, oozing blood, worms crawling from his mouth as he screams.

He's no longer out on the dark street but standing on a desk in my classroom, with The Dragon yelling at him to get down, while Connor bursts in with a gun and sprays everyone with red paint.

Only it isn't paint, it's blood. Splashing onto the walls, dripping down the windows, forming puddles on the floor. Puddles that grow until the classroom is one huge red lake of kids thrashing around, drowning.

And it's not supposed to be like this. It's all wrong. It's me that's bleeding. Drowning in my own blood that's flooding my throat.

My body suddenly thrusts forward, pulling me back inside it, so I see the gush of vomit spray into the grey cardboard bowl, that someone's holding in front of my mouth. My eyes won't focus but I know this isn't any railway station. This is a bed. A hospital, I think. But is it real?

'Josie?'

The voice sounds real enough. A familiar voice. A voice that draws me back, makes me look at the frizzy blonde hair, the plump face.

'Mum?' I say.

'It's Moira, Josie.'

I try not to let the hurt show as the face comes into full view. Grey hair, not blonde. Far too old. My eyes start darting round the room like they're out on their own. I can't control them.

They're looking for him.

But they find only the small hospital room. The metal cabinet. The sink in the corner. Moira sitting on the edge of the bed.

'Where is he?' I ask.

'Who?'

'Barry.'

'Barry?' says Moira.

'He got away, didn't he? He got away!'

'You've been shouting out in your sleep,' Moira says. 'You've been having a nightmare.'

'That wasn't part of the dream,' I say. 'It was Barry. Barry who stabbed me.'

'Nobody stabbed you, Josie,' she says, looking genuinely confused.

My hands go to my chest, my stomach, my ribs.

There's no wound. No blood. No bandages.

'On the station,' I say. 'Barry. He stabbed me. I couldn't have dreamt that. I couldn't have. There was someone following me. I turned round. It was him. It was Barry.'

Moira stares at me for a moment, taking it in. Working it out.

'The man who bumped into you was called Gordon Watson,' she says quietly. 'He was the same man who called for the ambulance when you fell. He happens to have tattoos, Josie. Rather a lot of them. But otherwise he doesn't look much like Barry. You must have panicked, Josie. You never saw past the tattoos.'

'But—'

Then I realize. None of this is real. It's all part of the dream. I'm still lying on that platform. I must be.

'Josie. come on now. Sit up again. Don't go back to sleep,' says Moira, pressing a button at the side of the bed. 'You've been out for over two hours.' A nurse comes in. Gives me a sip of water. Then a tablet. Then another sip of water, which I swill round my mouth. Tasting it, feeling it. Trying to touch reality.

'The man you bumped into tried to hold you, steady

123

you,' Moira tells me, as soon as the nurse has gone. 'But you kicked him, pulled away from him. Not so much fell over, as passed out, he said.'

'There was no knife?' I say, clutching Moira's hand.

'No knife,' Moira confirms.

'No Barry?'

'Only in your mind, Josie.'

That's the trouble though, isn't it? I'm not so much in my mind as out of it, most of the time.

Even Moira got a bit stressed by my latest freak-out. Got the doctor to increase my pills a bit and arranged for me to have some extra counselling sessions with the shrink.

They started in the Easter holiday and they're going to run all through this summer term. To help see me through my exams. I've missed a lot of time, a lot of work but they won't take that into account. College doesn't know about my past, my problems. My whole application form was a lie, apart from my qualifications. A form filled in while my social worker stood over me, making sure I didn't make any mistakes, reveal any secrets. I had false school reports, false home address – even a nice make-believe family!

So to college, I'm just an ordinary student and if I don't pass my exams they might chuck me out. And I don't want that.

College is a bit of a stress but it's all I've got really which is why I keep lying to Moira and the shrink. So they won't try to stop me from going.

124

I tell them I'm OK now. That their talks and tablets are doing the trick. I don't tell them about the feelings I get. That I'm still being followed.

That's all they are. Feelings. Paranoia. I know that now, which is why I can handle it. On my own.

And I don't tell them that you've surfaced again, Alex. Because I can handle that too. I won't let you take over. I won't.

What I can't handle though, is being too involved, constantly having to think about what I'm saying. So I've pulled back a bit from the college crowd. Maybe go out once a week, that's all. And if they think I'm a bit of a swot, staying in, revising for my exams, well that's fine by me.

At first, Soppy Sarah laughed at me having my lunch on my own in the library but she soon got bored. Besides, I'm not on my own most days now because Mark comes and joins me. You're not allowed to talk in our college library, which suits me just fine. So Mark and I sit, eating our sandwiches, reading our books.

Mark's not good looking like Graham but he's not exactly ugly either. Sort of ordinary really. Average height, average build, light brown hair in no particular style. It just sort of flops around, doing its own thing. Nice smile though and lovely teeth. Ridiculously white, even teeth, like film stars have.

We talk on our way to and from the library, of course, and it'd only need a bit of encouragement for him to ask me out. Only I don't reckon I'll bother because the other

125

day we got talking about what we wanted to do when we leave and Mark said he'd like to become a dog handler in the police force, eventually.

Not a good idea, getting involved with a future cop! But Mark, the student, is OK as a friend.

I've had a bit of a blow to my own future plans too. My probation officer tells me I might not be able to work in zoos. Too many children around.

'That's stupid,' I told her. 'I'm not gonna harm anybody, am I? What do they think I'm going to do? Lay into the kiddies with a pitchfork.'

She wasn't impressed by my outburst. Looked as though she believed that's exactly what I might do. But she said she'd look into it properly for me.

I mean, it's crazy, isn't it? I know I'm not allowed to work with children directly. I couldn't be a nursery nurse or anything, even if I wanted to. But you can't avoid kids totally, can you? I'll probably want kids of my own one day. Or will I?

Part of me does. The Josie part. But I'm scared that, under enough pressure, Alex might break through again. Totally. Do something crazy. End up inside again and that wouldn't be any good for a kid, would it? Being taken into care or something 'cos its mum was locked away.

Or, even worse…what if I turned on the kid…but no. I couldn't hurt a kid. I'm sure I couldn't.

Not now. Not if I was me. Not if I was in control. But what if the hallucinations took over?

Oh boy, not a good time to be thinking about it. I've

got an exam this afternoon. The good news is that it's the last one. The bad news is that it's biology, my worst subject. Trying to remember all those confusing bits and pieces, tubes, organs, bones. Trouble is, the practicals, the dissections, tend to make me sick so I don't exactly concentrate and I'm left trying to figure it out from the diagrams in the books.

Timing my entrance into the exam hall is a bit tricky. But I've got it down to a fine art now. Not too early so I don't have to be crushed in the swirling crowds with Soppy Sarah screaming down my ear.

'Oh I'm so nervous. I'm going to fail. I know I'm going to fail.'

Not so late that I'm the last one in and everybody turns to stare.

Even though I get the timing right, it's still scary. Hall full of people sitting in silence, the only sound is the papers flopping face down on the desk and someone opening all the windows. Good job 'cos it's boiling in here. And I daren't roll my sleeves up in case someone sees the scars.

Typical, isn't it? You can always rely on a heat wave during exam fortnight.

Sweat's already starting to drip off my forehead and it's almost a relief when the invigilator tells us to start. More than a relief when I see the first question. Grouping animals into the right species and sub species. I can do that.

The next couple of questions are OK. There're a few

I'm not happy with at all and number 5 I just know I'll have to leave till the end.

It's a diagram of the digestive system of a rabbit and by the time I get back to it I've only got ten minutes left. Ten minutes to remember what goes where and how it all links up.

And it had to be a rabbit, didn't it? Splayed open like that. Even a diagram can make me retch. I like my animals alive, these days, not dead.

The first animal you . . . Gemma . . . I . . . was introduced to in the therapy centre at the unit was a rabbit, called Cola.

Jet black. Very small. Very friendly. A beginner's rabbit. The sort of rabbit who didn't much care if you handled him a bit rough at first. Not 'cos he was stupid or anything. He wasn't. He was dead smart. Used to open the food cupboard by sticking his paw in and pulling, so they had to put a lock on it in the end.

But he was very trusting too. So people-friendly that he'd hop after you, if you didn't pick him up, follow you around like a little dog. And it didn't matter to me that he was the same with everyone. Somehow, to me, he was my rabbit.

What I didn't realize at the time was that Cola was already quite old. Because you can't tell so easily with animals, can you? They don't have wrinkles, glasses or walking sticks, do they? And when they finally age, it happens quite suddenly.

With Cola it was losing a couple of teeth and then, one day, his back legs went. He couldn't move them. And

I remember screaming when I saw him trying to pull himself along, gripping the floor of his cage with his two front feet.

The vet shook his head but he gave Cola an injection and it seemed to do the trick. When I left him in his cage that Thursday afternoon he seemed fine again. But he died in the night.

I wouldn't believe them when they told me. I wanted to see him. Wanted to see for myself. So they unfastened the white bin liner, the plastic shroud that they'd wrapped him in and let me look. They let me choose the spot in the garden where we buried him.

And I'll never forget that day in the garden. Insisting we put a carrot beside his cold, rigid body. Knowing he'd never eat it. That it would rot in that hole just like he would. That it was over. Final. Finished.

I'd been in the unit eight months when Cola died. I was twelve years old. And that night I cut myself for the first time.

A hand's reaching down, wrestling my pen away from me. The pen that's been stabbing into my arm. Miss Layton points the pen at the paper. Not random pointing but hints. Hints about which labels go with which bits.

She's bending the rules because she thinks my stabbing is exam nerves. She puts the pen back in my hand and looks at the clock. Two minutes. I can get half of it done, if I'm quick.

Then I'm out of there. Hanging around at the end is even worse than hanging around at the start. Everyone analysing what they've done. Faces turning pale as people like Sarah tell us what we should have put.

Besides, I've got a reason to be back early tonight because it's Moira's birthday. We're not going out or anything because Moira hasn't been feeling too good. One of those summer colds that won't go away and has settled on her chest. She's prone to colds and chest infections, is Moira, so Frank said it was best if she didn't go out and he's bringing in a Chinese. Moira's favourite.

There were loads of cards delivered for her this morning. But I haven't given her mine yet. Or the present. And me and Lara have clubbed together for some champagne. The proper stuff. The expensive stuff.

Moira's children all live miles away. Mega miles, as in America and New Zealand, so she's stuck with us to help her celebrate and me and Lara want to make it special. Dress the table up nice with flowers and candles.

So I hurry across the quad, trying to ignore the footsteps behind me. Real or hallucination. Who can tell these days?

'Josie!' someone shouts out.

The voice sounds real enough, strong enough, so I turn round.

Mr Phinn. What does he want?

'Well done,' he says, scurrying towards me, wiping his face with a white hankie.

'Sorry?'

'Your result. You must have seen it. I put them up at lunchtime.'

He's been quick. We only did his paper last Tuesday.

'86 per cent,' he says. 'Top mark. Brilliant.'

My face is burning so much, I have to get away.

Top. Me. 86 per cent. Top. Better than Graham. Better than Mark. Better than Sarah. Top. 86 per cent.

The words spin round and round in my head all the way home like some mad religious chant, pushing away the doubts. It's only one result. There's nothing to say I'll do as well in the rest. Maybe Mr Phinn has got me mixed up with someone else. Maybe he's added the marks up wrong.

But maybe not. Maybe I'm really top. Me. 86 per cent.

It's amazing how good something like this can make me feel about myself. It felt pretty good being Gemma getting her GCSEs. Her A-levels. Even though they were fairly average grades. Nothing like this. Not 86 per cent. Not top. I don't think I've ever been top in anything in my life. Or in Gemma's life. Certainly not in Alex's life. Unless you count the football and The Dragon's awards.

There's a girls' football team at college and I've been tempted a few times but I don't reckon I'd be any good now. It's been too long since I played. We didn't do team sports in the unit. Too dangerous. Too many volatile tempers. And most of the girls weren't that interested in sport anyway so I just played a bit of badminton and tennis with the staff.

I still like watching football but, thinking about it, I wouldn't want to play anymore because it's too much part of then and I have to concentrate on now.

Now I'm Josie, jogging down the street, full of my news. Planning to tell Moira over our special meal. Knowing I won't be able to wait that long. It's going to burst out the minute I see her.

Me. Top. 86 . . .

My chant grinds to a sudden halt as I see the ambulance.

Not my house. Please don't let it be my house.

But it is. Two paramedics are carrying a stretcher down the path.

'Moira,' I shout as I break into a run.

Chapter 13

Moira's chest wheezes as she follows the stretcher down the path. I can hear it even before I reach the gate, even before I see Lara lying there, eyes shut, face totally white, screwed-up in pain.

And I feel the pain too. I really do. It starts in my head, slashing down, zigzagging through my body, like it's ripping me apart.

'She fell down the stairs,' Moira says, her face almost as pale and drawn as Lara's. 'She was all set to feed the ducks before you came home, but she was so excited about my birthday, she didn't know what to do first. Decided to go upstairs and fetch my present. Next thing I know there's a crash. Must have tripped at the top. Fell the full length of them, I think.'

Moira's voice sounds more panicky than I've ever heard it before.

'She was lying at a funny angle,' Moira whispers. 'Couldn't move. Couldn't move at all. I think she might have broken something. I think she might have broken her back.'

A groan comes from Lara and I reach down to touch her hand before they start to lift her into the ambulance. She's clutching something, which she's trying to hold out to me.

'It's the bread,' says Moira, starting to cry.

I've never seen Moira cry before and it sets me off too.

'The bread for her ducks,' Moira says. 'She dropped my present but she held onto her bread.'

'Will you feed them, Josie?' Lara says, real quietly so I can barely hear.

''Course.'

'Promise?'

'Promise,' I say, taking the bag as her eyes close again.

'I've phoned Frank,' Moira says, wiping her eyes, slipping into her business-like mode. 'He'll be home soon. Then maybe you and him can come to the hospital.'

'Can't I come now? With you?'

'Best if I go on my own, for now,' she says.

I don't want to be on my own. Moira knows that. But I can see she needs to focus on Lara so I smile. Nod at her. Try to be brave.

'Remember,' says Moira, 'you've got those ducks to feed. You promised Lara. But make sure you lock up, eh? Take your mobile and I'll keep in touch.'

There're a few other instructions too but nothing really registers because the ambulance doors are closing and I'm left standing on the street as they drive off, bag of bread in my hand, tears still streaming down my face.

I go inside. Dump my college stuff. I know I can dump the bag of bread too. In the bin. Lara will never know. But she'll ask.

Whatever's happened to her and whatever state she's in, I know she'll ask about her ducks.

And I won't be able to lie to Lara. Crazy, isn't it? My whole life's one bloody enormous lie but I won't be able to look into Lara's eyes and tell her I've fed her precious ducks if I haven't.

Besides, what else is there to do? Except sit and fret and wait. Pull the house apart looking for scissors. And Moira doesn't want any of that right now, Josie, OK? She's got enough to worry about.

So I lock up and set off for the park, the long way round. Me and bridges just aren't going to work today.

It's turned six o'clock. It's still pretty hot and people are trying to catch the last of the sunshine, sprawled out on their lawns, sitting outside pubs, strolling towards the park. But they're not going to be there much longer because the clouds are coming over and I've just heard the first rumble of thunder, I think.

Funny how the weather can change so quickly. Like feelings, I guess. All that euphoria I felt about my exam. Gone. Meaningless. What does it matter with Lara on her way to hospital?

I don't know why I care about Lara, but I do. The realization shocks me. I don't want to care about her. I don't want to care about anybody. Because it *hurts*. Hurts so much that I slam the park gates as I go through. Kick an empty Coke can. A stone. Anything I can find.

There's a fair on in the park. I see the big wheel first, before I hear the music. Happy music. Mocking music.

And, for a minute I think it's not thunder and lightning looming, it's the flashing lights and heavy bass beat. Nice thought but one of those huge drops of summer rain splashes down my neck, spoiling the illusion.

Time to get moving but having approached the park from the far side I have to more or less go through the fair to get to the lake.

And fairs have this sort of hypnotic effect on me. Always have had. When I was a kid, when I was Alex, I used to go to fairs a lot. With my mum when I was really little 'cos she loved fairs, did my mum.

Then, when I was a bit older, I'd go on my own or with my mates. Even fancied working in a fairground, at one time, I remember. I suppose they struck me as wild, exotic, dangerous places back then. Not the run-down, dirty junk yard that this one seems to be.

It's got those fantastic fairground smells though. Fried onion, sizzling burgers, toffee apple...Not that I'm hungry right now but I love the smells. Apart from the sweet, sickly stink of candyfloss. I hate candyfloss. I used to love it when I was little but I hate it now.

The rides are all going but it's not very busy. The lull between the parents and kiddies of the afternoon going home and the teenage hordes of the evening arriving, I guess.

So I mooch around, finding more things to kick – sweet wrappers, beer cans. Trying to ignore the increasing spots of rain. Kicking the cans hard. Anger management it's called. You can kick and punch objects. Not people.

Why am I angry? Because that's the way hurt always comes out with me. In anger. And because it's not fair. It's not fair that Lara's lying there in hospital. That she might end up in a bloody wheelchair. That it all had to happen on Moira's birthday.

'Three darts for a pound,' a bored stallholder calls out to me.

But I wouldn't trust myself with darts.

So I stand staring at the waltzer whizzing round, making my head spin along with it. There's nobody on it apart from the little blond kid and her mum. But even they're not real.

It's you, isn't it, Alex? With your mum on the waltzer when you were about five years old. Laughing and shrieking so she didn't see how scared you were.

Not that she'd have seen anyway. She was having a great time and all she saw was the lad who was spinning our carriage round. The attendant with the long, dark hair and thick, fake gold chains.

Later, when the fair was closed up, you sat in the dark, on the steps of the waltzer, eating the candyfloss your mum had given you. Candyfloss which tasted damp and salty from your tears.

'What are you crying for?' your mum asked, when she came back. 'Told you I wouldn't be long, didn't I? Bet I haven't been gone longer than half an hour, have I?'

Maybe not. But it felt longer. Much longer.

She picked you up, gave you a cuddle, made you believe everything was all right. You fell asleep in her arms and when you woke up, you were back in your own bed, with the remains of the candyfloss stuck hard round your face so it hurt when you tried to shout out.

Nobody knows about that. I haven't ever told anybody about how Mum left me alone in a fairground, late at night. I haven't let on about a lot of things. What's the point? Mum never meant to hurt me, to frighten me. She loved me. Didn't she? At least I think she did, back then.

I loved her, anyway. I still do.

And the things that happened sometimes, the bad things, they weren't her fault, were they? I get really mad when I think back to the trial sometimes. When I think about what my defence people said. How they tried to make out like it was my mum's fault or something. Saying she didn't know how to look after a kid properly.

'How could she?' they said. 'What sort of family life had she ever known? She'd been in care herself since she was seven.'

It was true. She had been in care. So what? Loads of kids grow up in care. Like Lara. It's no big deal. It doesn't make them bad people, does it?

Mum used to tell me bits about it sometimes and I wish I'd listened better. I wish I could remember more about what happened. How she felt. But I don't. I don't remember much at all, except that her mum, the gran I never knew, just disappeared one day. Left five kids and never came back. Mum's dad couldn't cope and one by one the kids were taken into care. First the girls. Then the three lads. Mum told me all their names once but I've forgotten.

Social services kept all the kids in touch with each other

138

for a while. They'd all get together for weekend visits with their dad. But then he stopped turning up and it all sort of fell apart. The kids got moved from foster home to foster home. Two of the little ones got adopted eventually. But Mum reckoned nobody wanted her. Said she'd been with five or six families. None of them could cope with her for long, especially when she got into her teens.

'I was a bit of a handful,' she used to tell me, 'but I turned out all right in the end, didn't I?'

She did too. And that's the point. She was all right was my mum. It wasn't her fault I turned out the way I did. She lost everything because of me.

One of her dreams, one of the things she used to talk about when she was happy, was tracing her birth family again one day. Her dad, her brothers and sister. Maybe even trying to track down her mum. She used to get quite excited about it and the first few times she mentioned it, I got excited too, thinking about having a gran and grandad, aunties and uncles, like my mates at school had. Looking at a few old photographs. Listening to Mum say how easy it'd be. All she'd have to do was get in touch with social services.

But she never did. Don't know whether she ever will. Whether she has.

Probably best not to, I reckon. Especially not the way things are now. What could she tell them? What could she say? Besides, it's no good looking back all the time, is it? Wishing things had been different. Wishing you could start over.

Listen to yourself, Josie! What are you saying? What do you think you're doing yourself? Now. Right at this moment?

But this is what happens when I get worked up. I don't exactly set out to delve into the past. It comes sweeping back of its own accord, like some great tidal wave and I can't stop it. There's nothing I can do. And all the time the waltzer's spinning round and my head's spinning with it but I can't stop watching.

Come on, Moira. Phone, can't you? Tell me what's happening. Give me something to do. Something else to think about.

Why the hell hasn't she phoned? They must have reached the hospital by now. She must know I'm worried.

No phone, that's why. Idiot! No matter how many times I pat my trouser pockets, I don't feel anything because it isn't there. It's still in my college bag on the hall floor. When Moira specially told me to take it with me, didn't she?

How did people ever manage without mobiles? I feel completely lost without mine. Isolated. Stranded. Naked almost.

It gives me the push I need, though, to tear myself away, to get home. Moira'll be frantic if she's trying to get through and can't reach me.

If I hurry up and feed the ducks, if I can talk myself into going the quick way home, across the bridge, I can be back in fifteen minutes. Less if I run. Even then, I'm going to get soaked 'cos the rain's coming down pretty heavy now.

The lake's right over the other side. And it's pretty funny passing the kiddies' play area, the tennis courts and the putting green because there're all these people in shorts with their T-shirts pulled up over their heads, running for cover, scurrying home. Looking nervously at trees as sheets of lightning open up.

'British weather, eh?' someone mutters as they pass. 'Talk about changeable.'

It's not only the weather that's unpredictable though, is it? It's life. Love it or loathe it, you can't trust it. That's what I reckon, anyway.

'Quack, quack, quack . . .'

The ducks start gathering round the edge of the lake and they sound like they're laughing. Well, it's all right for them, isn't it? With their waterproof feathers.

I can see why Lara likes them though. They're dead sweet and sort of cheerful. Excitable. Friendly.

The quacking gets louder as I chuck the whole bagful of bread in the water. So loud that it takes a moment for the other sound to filter through.

'Mummy! Mummy! Mummy!'

I look round peering through rain that's so heavy now, it's almost solid. A torrent of water obscuring my view of the blond kid, standing further down, by the end of the lake's edge.

Not a real kid, of course. It can't be. Because I'm sure it wasn't there a minute ago when I looked.

It must be you. You when you were five. But it doesn't look like you. Because, even then, even when you were five, you never wore girly dresses. It was always trousers, shorts, dungarees and stuff. You'd scream blue murder if your mum tried to put a dress on you.

'Mummy! Mummy!'

The girl who's screaming is wearing a dress. Short. Blue and white spotty thing, clinging to her, wet and dripping.

This is crazy. I know this is crazy as I move towards her. I know she's not going to be real.

But instead of evaporating, her image gets stronger, more solid as I approach. The scream gets louder, so it's really doing my head in. Like big time.

She's nothing like you close up. She's got freckles. Lots of freckles. Her eyes are hazel. Wide open. Terrified. Even her hair is more ginger than blond.

'Mummy! I want Mummy!'

What the hell do I do? I look around. There's nobody, but nobody, left in the park. At least not as far as I can see.

Leave it, Josie. Walk away. She's not your problem. You can do without all this right now. You have to get home. Find out how Lara is.

But the kid's dangerously close to the edge of the water and she's working herself up into a right state.

OK, so think, Josie. You're frightening the kid, just standing here like this. Make-up streaked, mascara running in your eyes. Hair plastered all over your face. You must look like something nasty that's just escaped from the ghost train.

142

Say something. Speak quietly. Calm her down.

'It's OK. Mummy's not far. She'll be back soon.'

'I want my mummy! I want my mummy!'

Oh, my God! Some instinct, some reflex I didn't know I had makes me reach out and grab her as she stumbles towards the water.

Then I know she's real because she kicks out at me, catching my ankle, digging her tiny nails into my arm. She's obviously been warned about stranger danger.

But I hold on, praying that no one comes. Not right now. What would they think? If they saw me holding onto her like this?

'Listen,' I say. 'Listen to me. I'm Josie. Mummy sent me to find you. I'm going to take you back to her. OK?'

She goes sort of limp as I hold her. Stops screaming, like she's suddenly exhausted. And for a second I'm terrified that I've squeezed the life right out of her. But no. She's breathing. Heavily. Unevenly. But she's fine.

'OK,' I say, loosening my grip slowly, making sure she can stand up on her own. 'I'm Josie. I'm Mummy's friend. I'm going to help you to find her.'

She grabs my hand. Holds it tight. Like she trusts me. Or like she knows I'm the only thing she's got right now.

'OK,' I say again. 'What's your name?'

'Amy.'

'And I'm Josie, OK?'

'Josie,' she repeats.

'Right, so where was Mummy...?'

The minute I start to ask, I know I'm not going to get

143

an answer. Amy's lip starts to quiver and her head starts shaking.

Mistake. I shouldn't have asked. I'm supposed to know! I'm the one in control.

'It's all right,' I say. 'I know where to find her.'

No point wandering round the park or Amy's going to freak out again, if we don't find her mum. Best just head for the police station. Hand her over there. They'll know what to do. Chances are, her mum will have reported her missing already. The police might even be out looking.

Oh, shit! They mustn't find me with her. Like I've abducted her or something. The mere suspicion would be enough to get me locked up again. I don't have to commit a crime. Don't have to be charged with anything. Being found with a strange kid like this would be enough. I know it would.

Get her handed over, Josie, and quick. The police station isn't far beyond the bridge. Shove her inside. Say she was lost. Leave before they can ask too many questions.

The bridge isn't just any old bridge though, is it? It's a pedestrian bridge. Over a busy road which runs in front of this side of the park.

You're going to have to cross it, Josie. Cross it with a child. Hear the traffic racing along underneath. Hear the voices.

'Get him down, Alex. Get him down.'

Don't stop. You'll frighten her if you stop. You're in control. You're supposed to know where you're going. What you're doing.

This is now, Josie. Not then. Ignore the voices. They can't hurt you. Ignore the screams, the squeal of brakes. They're not real, Josie. They're in your head. From before. So walk quickly. Keep going. Keep hold of her hand. And don't look down. Whatever you do, Josie, don't look down.

Chapter 14

I freeze. Halfway across the bridge, I freeze. I can't go on and I can't go back. The rain's eased off a bit but there's no one around. No one to help.

Amy's tugging at my hand. She's soaked through, shivering, starting to cry again.

'Mummy, Mummy...'

Don't do that, Amy. Please don't do that. This is bad enough without you screaming, without you tearing my head apart. You don't know who you're with, Amy. You don't know what I might do. What I'm capable of. I barely know myself, if the voices close in on me.

Why can't I move? It's like I'm stuck in some sort of time warp, the sound of the traffic, the voices, holding me fast.

Amy tugs at my hand again. Urgently, desperately.

'I want my mummy!'

And I know just how she feels.

Before I know what I'm doing, I'm picking her up, holding her close. Propelling myself forward.

Not stopping when I reach the end of the bridge. Hurrying down the ramp at the other side, turning sharp left, then right until the police station's in front of us.

'A nice policeman's going to help you now,' I tell the girl.

Nice policeman! How have I ever managed to put those two words together? After what I went through with the cops. But this isn't for me. This is for Amy. So I repeat the words. Trying to keep my voice normal, balanced, rational.

Because it's not over. I've got to take her inside. And who knows who could be in there? Solicitors, probation officers, social workers. *My* probation officer, my social worker. Someone who might recognize me, question what I was doing with a child at all.

At least Amy's stopped crying. I put her down. Push open the door. Grab her hand and take her inside.

We don't get far. There's a young couple by the desk, the woman wild and hysterical, screaming at the desk sergeant.

'I don't want to answer any more bloody questions! I've told you. She disappeared! One minute she was with us and the next... Amy! Oh, my God, you're safe, you're safe!'

As soon as Amy leaves go of my hand, I'm out of there. It's done. Over. Almost. I've not even reached the corner when someone rushes up behind me, grabs my arm.

It's the guy from the police station. Amy's dad?

'Hey, wait,' he says, as I shake him off. 'You didn't even give us time to say thank you.'

'No need,' I say, edging away.

He mistakes my sharpness for disapproval, I guess, because he starts explaining.

'We'd come down to the park for a picnic tea,' he said.

'Had to pack up in a hurry when it started to rain. Shoved everything into the bags. Picked them up. Looked round. And she wasn't there. Amy wasn't there! We'd only taken our eyes off her for a couple of seconds. She doesn't usually wander off and we thought... oh, God, the things that went through our minds! All the nutters you read about these days.'

And he doesn't know he's looking one right in the eyes.

'If anything had happened to Amy...' he says.

Letting the words hang unfinished. Not knowing what they're doing to me. Because it's not him I'm hearing anymore. It's other people. Other families who weren't so lucky. Who lost their loved ones that day because of what you did, Alex.

'Thank you,' he says, suddenly clutching my hand. 'My wife and I... you know... I don't want to insult you or anything... I know you wouldn't expect anything... but we'd like to do something... to say thank you...'

He's let go of my hand and he's reaching inside his pocket, bringing out a wallet.

'No!' I say, moving away. 'No!'

'At least tell me your name,' he calls after me.

'I'm Josie,' I shout back. 'I'm Josie!'

Maybe one day, I'll be able to look back and feel good about what I did today. Moira says I should write all these things down. All the little things that make me feel better about myself. All the little signs that I'm moving on.

But I don't want to think about the future or the past. I want to concentrate on the here and now. Try to get home as fast as I can. Find out about Lara.

I'm almost at the corner of our street, about to cross over, when the car pulls up at the kerb.

'Where've you been?' Frank yells at me. 'Moira's been trying to phone you. Come on, get in.'

Frank used to scare me a bit at first, till I got used to him. 'Cos he's got this really loud voice which makes him sound angry, even when he's not.

'Look at you, you're soaked through,' he booms. 'And you look terrible!'

Bit of a flatterer, is Frank!

'Do you want to go home, get changed first, before we go to the hospital?' he asks.

'No,' I say. 'Just stick the heater on. I'll soon dry out. How is she? How's Lara?'

His face relaxes into a smile and I know it's OK. It's all going to be all right.

First week of the summer holidays and we've finally got our trip to the zoo. Moira and I wrestle poor Lara out of the car and into her wheelchair. One leg normal, the other stuck out, rigid in plaster. White plaster that's covered in get well messages and silly cartoon drawings that Frank's done.

Lara insists that I push her and sends Moira off to buy bags of food to feed some of the animals. A broken leg's not a lot of fun but Lara makes the best of it, like she always does and it could have been a whole lot worse.

Poor Moira had the social services on the doorstep the day after Lara's accident. Bloody cheek! As if Moira didn't have enough to cope with without filling in their stupid forms and answering a whole load of questions, like they were accusing her of negligence or something.

'It has to be done, Josie,' Moira said calmly when I lost my rag and started mouthing off.

But I was scared, wasn't I? Scared that they'd decide Moira was unfit. That Lara and me would get moved on somewhere. And I didn't want that. No way. I'm not stupid. I know I'll have to move on sometime. Manage on my own. But not yet, not till I've finished college.

With all the upset, I never did get to tell Moira about my exam. Not till we got the sheet with all my results on, anyway. I'd made a bit of a pig's mess of the biology but the rest were all right. More than all right, Moira said and, of course, she was dead pleased about Mr Phinn's course. Me coming top.

'It's scratching its bum!' Lara squeals in fits of hysterical laughter. 'Look at that monkey scratching its bum!'

The monkey looks offended and scurries off up a rope, swinging around the wooden climbing frame, slithering back down the rope, hurling itself at the wire mesh of the cage, gripping on, grinning at us.

And I can't help grinning back. A keeper passes, pushing a wheelbarrow full of fruit and vegetables.

That's going to be me one day! My probation officer actually did as promised and checked out whether I was allowed to work in zoos. It seems I am. As long as I don't do anything stupid, of course. Break any of the rules of my probation.

Which is why I haven't told anybody about what happened that day in the park, with Amy. Not even Moira. 'Cos I'm scared they might not understand. Might even think I was cracking up. Again! Fantasizing about rescuing children.

Sometimes I even wonder myself if it was a fantasy. Whether I made the whole thing up. I don't think so but it's possible. The mess my head's still in, anything's possible.

'Awww, look at that,' Lara says. 'Isn't it sweet!'

Mother elephant with her trunk curled round her offspring. Proud. Protective. That's how it's supposed to be, isn't it? Mothers and children? So what went wrong? Why didn't Lara's mother feel that way? Or mine?

Stop it, Josie. Stop it right now. This is supposed to be a fun day out not another session with the shrink.

I'm still seeing her. My psychiatrist, counsellor, whatever she is. Maybe I'll always have to. I don't know. Moira says there's no shame in it. Tells me some pop stars and film stars pay millions for therapy. That it's even sort of fashionable, these days!

Alison, at college, reckons she wants to be an animal psychologist. Says when she's done her basic course, she's going to go on for another few years. Get a degree.

Mr Phinn reckons I could do that if I wanted. Says I'm clever enough to do a higher course.

'You could still do zookeeping,' he tells me. 'Only

you'd start at a higher level. There'd be more chance of going on to be head-keeper. That sort of thing.'

'We can feed these!' Lara shouts out. 'We can feed anything in here.'

She's pointing to a gateway, leading to a section full of more docile animals who won't take your arm off if you offer them some food. So we wander round, Lara almost falling out of her wheelchair as she tries to feed some goats.

I don't know what Lara'll do when she finishes college. At the moment she's doing a sort of life skills course. Basic maths and English. A lot of practical stuff like cooking and home maintenance. Maybe she'll do something with animals eventually too. She'd be dead good.

'What about the tigers?' Lara shouts when the food bags are finally empty. 'We haven't seen the tigers yet or the giraffes or the lions or—'

Moira looks exhausted already so we leave her in the café, promising we'll be back in an hour for lunch.

'Ugh, they're kissing,' Lara shouts.

For a minute I think she's talking about the animals, but no. She's pointing to a bench where a couple of kids are all but eating each other.

'Do you do that with your boyfriend?' Lara giggles.

'Mark's a friend,' I tell her. 'Not a boyfriend. It's different.'

OK, so I've been a bit stupid. Seen him a couple of times on my own. Found out I liked him a whole lot more than I thought.

Told Moira a bit about him. Told my shrink too. Just to see. Just to test out the ground.

They both told me the same thing. It's early days yet, with Mark, so that's OK. But if I ever find myself getting really involved, if I ever want to settle down, get married, I'll have to tell. I'll have to tell my partner the truth.

Oh yeah, sure! What sort of person could survive that? Who could possibly love me, once they knew?

Even worse, if the relationship survived, if we had kids, would I have to tell them one day too? Would I have to tell them about you?

'You nearly tipped me out then!' Lara shouts, as I bump the chair over a verge.

'Sorry. I was thinking.'

'You're not supposed to be thinking,' Lara tells me. 'You're supposed to be looking at the animals.'

She's right, of course. Not a lot of point in thinking. I can't see Josie at forty, or thirty or even twenty, really. I don't know what sort of future she's got or even if she's got one at all.

So we move on, see the tigers and the giraffes, have lunch with Moira.

In the afternoon we follow the keepers around, listening to their talks as they feed the sealions, the penguins, the lions, the chimps. Taking it all in. It's brilliant. Really brilliant. I treat everyone to an ice-cream. A great big one with a chocolate flake in the top. And I don't ever remember enjoying a day as much as I've enjoyed today.

Moira and me are still chattering, laughing like a couple of school kids as we head back to the car, Lara spark out, asleep in her chair.

An old couple smile at us as they pass. Maybe to them we look like a family. Me, my mum and my sister. A game I know I've been playing all day. A stupid game, a childish game, but it makes me feel happy, so what the heck.

'Alex! Alex!'

Moira tenses beside me, so I know the cry is real.

I can't help it. I swing round. There's a little lad running full pelt down the path, his harassed parents screaming after him.

'Alex! Alex!'

The name screeches through my head like nails down a blackboard but I won't let it spoil the day. I won't. It's been a great day. One of the best ever. One I'll always remember, whatever happens.

We pause for a moment. Lara muttering in her sleep, Moira holding onto the wheelchair.

And me, staring over my shoulder, looking back. Like I always do. Like I guess I always will.